THE BOOK
of
EXPERT DRIVING

THE BOOK
of
EXPERT DRIVING

(Revised)

by E. D. Fales, Jr.

Foreword by John R. Whiting
Introduction by William J. Toth
Research Manager
Society of Automotive Engineers

HAWTHORN BOOKS
A division of Elsevier-Dutton
New York

3 4 5 6 7 8 9 10

ISBN: 0-8015-0808-8

FOREWORD: A REPORT FROM THE ROAD

THIS WILL BE UNLIKE ANY BOOK on driving you have ever seen or read, for several reasons.

First, it will be frankly controversial in spots, as in its discussion of left-foot braking, "side-contact" driving, and the use of emergency flares.

Second, it is a report on changing driver techniques, for it recognizes that some of the standard concepts are now old-fashioned and dangerous.

Third, it was not written in a laboratory or in a library. It was written, almost in its entirety, on the road.

This is a professional driver's book, not a racing driver's memoir and not a teacher's text—except that the many articles Ed Fales has written for national magazines have done a great deal to educate adult drivers.

The book came about, in most senses, because Fales is a specialist in writing about cars and driving. In one special sense this book happened because two men—Ed and I—were sitting in the cockpit of my boat one fall afternoon. We were comparing the mountain of technical information available in books and magazines about boating (sailing, piloting, navigating, water-skiing, fishing) with what has been published for the much larger group of automobile drivers who enjoy the cars they drive, enjoy the open road, and enjoy mastering the skills of car handling. We talked about that famous book, Chapman's *Piloting, Seamanship and Small Boat Handling,* and how there should be a book like it for drivers, and I joked: "Well, Ed, if you do the book you won't need a chapter on anchoring, but you will have to tell them about docking—I mean parallel parking."

For two decades, while many others have been theorizing about driving, Ed Fales has been out on the highway, experimenting, testing standard techniques, developing new ones. He has worked with excellent teams from several universities, and with the cooperation of top state authorities and the Armed Services (which are seriously interested in better driving). Much cooperation has generously been given him by the police of several states and cities.

He has run night tests to see how drivers can cope with headlight-glare problems. He has tested the actual performance of intoxicated drivers—under controlled conditions. Using radar he has found out the degree to which drivers do—and do not—slow down for emergency flares. With police help he has questioned that most troublesome of motorists, the "slow driver," to find out why he obstructs traffic.

To discover new snow-driving techniques the author has driven through Rocky Mountain blizzards with emergency crews to see how *they* keep going when ordinary drivers fail. At the other end of the nation Maine lumberjacks have shown him tricks they use for getting started in deep snow when other cars are stuck.

He has ridden with state police in pursuits up to 120 miles per hour at night and then interviewed the arrested drivers.

In one state, North Carolina, he was the first to discover, with police help, that police sirens simply cannot be heard by motorists under some circumstances—a discovery that surprised the police themselves. And also in North Carolina he was able to demonstrate with the help of that state's excellent highway engineers how much more can be done to illuminate dangerous night highways—not with costly electric lights but by generous use of reflective materials—on bridges, turns, curbstones, and posts.

In the Acknowledgments the author credits some of the many men, agencies, and institutions that have assisted him in his work—generously and often with great enthusiasm.

Much of the author's research was done originally for such driver-interested publications as the *Reader's Digest, McCall's, Better Homes & Gardens, Parade* (the Sunday newspaper weekly), *Popular Mechanics, Popular Science Monthly,* and *American Youth,* the General Motors magazine for teenage drivers.

Some of his findings have been distributed to Congress, and many have been reprinted by the Armed Forces for the use of enlisted men. Others have been printed by the National Safety Council.

So it happens that a book has been written that goes beyond driver education to the real enjoyment of the automobile as transportation. Like any serious book, it has other values. It will aid safety on the road, it will enable you to develop as a driver for many years to come, and it can give you the same mastery of your car that a sailor or motorboatman has of his boat.

—John R. Whiting, Manager
Motor Boating & Sailing Books

ACKNOWLEDGMENTS

THE AUTHOR IS INDEBTED to a large number of people for help during the many on-the-road studies of driver behavior that made this book possible. Many people, companies, and agencies have been involved. He wishes to express thanks, too, to the magazine editors who encouraged him in his fact-finding studies and who patiently edited and printed his reports.

The source roots of this book run deep in many directions. The first seeds were planted by Mr. John R. Whiting, publisher of *Motor Boating* magazine, who thought this book ought to be written and said so, and then coaxed it along for three years; by Mr. Jess Gorkin, the distinguished editor of *Parade,* the Sunday newspaper weekly, who first gave me a free hand to go out on the road and find out all I could about drivers; by Mr. Robert P. Crossley, editor of *Popular Mechanics,* who suggested many avenues of investigation; and by Mr. Ernest V. Heyn, editor of *Popular Science Monthly,* which printed many of my reports. All have graciously permitted certain material first written for them to be included in this book, as have, too, the editors of the *Reader's Digest,* who inspired Chapter IX.

For their encouragement the author also thanks the editors of *McCall's* and *American Youth,* the excellent Chevrolet magazine for young drivers.

Among those who have given active cooperation in many on-the-road studies for various magazines are: Assistant Professor William J. "Bill" Toth, of the New York University Safety Center; Michigan State University, the Harvard School of Public Health, the University of Michigan, Iowa State University, Purdue University, and the Highway Departments of Michigan, North Carolina, and California, and especially the snow experts of the Colorado Highway Department; the New York Thruway Authority and its deputy executive director, Mr. Philip Lee; Mr. Paul Burke, of the Maryland State Traffic Commission; Dr. Nathaniel H. Pulling, automotive-safety project director for Liberty Mutual Insurance Company, and Mr. Robert F. Daley, skid-control consultant for the same company; the accident-investigation teams of State Farm Mutual Insurance Company and the excellent driver-education experts of the Aetna Casualty & Surety Company; the North Carolina Highway Patrol and the State Police of Connecticut, New York, Pennsylvania, Delaware, Maryland, Georgia, Michigan and New Jersey, all of whom cooperated in endless hours of road work; and the Baltimore City Police.

Harold L. Smith, driver-behavior consultant to the Ford Motor Company, the Bell System, and United Parcel; the engineers of NASA (the National Aeronautics and Space Administration), who were first to discover that tires hydroplane in rain; the National Safety Council's various experts, including the able Mr. Jack Horner; the American Automobile Association's staff in Washington, D.C., and the Michigan Motor Club; Dr. Richard M. Michaels, former science adviser to the U.S. Bureau of Public Roads; Dr. Donald A. Gordon, psychologist in that bureau and in the U. S. Department of Transportation; Dr. James Schuster, of Villanova University, formerly of Purdue University; and Mr. David H. Buswell, of the National Highway Research Board.

Professor of Highway Engineering Harold L. Michael, of Purdue; Professor Milton E. Harr, of Purdue; Professor J. C. Oppenlander, formerly of Purdue, now Chairman of Civil Engineering at the University of Vermont; Dr. Merrill J. Allen, of Indiana University; Mr. John Fitch, automotive consultant and former sports-car racing champion; Dr. John O. Moore, Safety Coordinator, New York State Motor Vehicle Department, and first director of the famous Cornell Crash Injury Research Project; the tire-test teams of the Goodyear Tire & Rubber Company; the Detroit Traffic Safety Association; Minnesota Mining & Manufacturing Company; Insurance Information Institute; Dr. Alfred L. Moseley, traffic psychologist, and the American Trial Lawyers Association.

Dr. Donald Buck and other safety experts and officers of the U.S. Armed Forces, who have distributed many of the author's reports to servicemen; Mr. Robert Gregory, driver-education instructor at the Housatonic Valley Regional High School in Connecticut, who gave critical advice; Mr. Herbert Shuldiner, associate editor of *Popular Science Monthly*.

And finally, thanks to my wife, Edwina, who, like Managing Editor Grace Bechtold, of Bantam Books, had to live with this book in the months during which it was written.

—E. D. F., Jr.

Falls Village, Conn., 1970

CONTENTS

PART THREE. DRIVING UNDER DANGEROUS CONDITIONS

LIST OF ILLUSTRATIONS

INTRODUCTION

YOU CANNOT READ THIS BOOK and honestly say you did not learn something. No matter who you are—an experienced driver, a new one, a professional fleet driver, or even a teacher of driving—you will find that this book will add a new dimension to your driving. Filled with new road-proven ideas, investigated by the author, the following pages go beyond any text or guide you have ever read. There is no theory here. There is knowledge supported by practical road investigations. Thousands of people driving millions of miles have contributed to this book. To check the reliability and practicality of the information herein, the author traveled thousands of miles himself in the last twenty years. He discovered numerous new techniques in traffic safety that he records here for you. Over the years many of the author's writings were the basis for changes in our present traffic picture. In this book he lets you sit behind your steering wheel using his rich experience and the eyes of an expert to guide you.

—William J. Toth
Research Manager
Society of Automotive Engineers

PART ONE

THE FINE POINTS
OF CAR HANDLING

CHAPTER I

THE THREE GREAT PRINCIPLES

THERE ARE MORE THAN 100 million drivers in the United States. Most of them have average skill. But a small, passionate group are experts and experience the full joy of operating the fine mechanism of an automobile, enjoying the pace of the road and the convenience of personal transportation. They leave the anguish and frustrations of driving to the amateurs.

Safety is a great by-product of expert driving because it is the amateur who makes the mistakes that result in money- and life-wasting accidents. What distinguishes the expert from the inept are three great principles:

1. Good driving is a quiet art, never a cheap or showy skill. The expert knows that noisy or flashy driving is a sign of ineptness.
2. A good driver can handle emergencies.
3. An expert driver needs a good car. A driver can't be at his best if his equipment isn't topnotch also.

If your car is not really handling and performing well, get rid of it if an overhaul won't correct the fault. Buy a good car.

What is a good car? First, it looks good—clean and solid. Animal experts admire the conformation and stance of a fine horse. A fine car must have these too. It must look solid and well-balanced on its wheels. It must have form, or it will not ride well. And it must handle well, respond instantly and precisely. It must not droop, sway, sag, falter, or lean the wrong way when running.

It need not be an expensive car. If you drive an average amount, about 12,000 miles a year, mostly around town, with one or two long trips, it need not even be a new one. If you drive 15,000 to 25,000 or more miles a year—with a good deal of mileage on superhighways—a fairly new car is advisable. An older car can be made to give you superior handling qualities but often at much expense.

For the high mileage driver a new car is not an extravagance but almost a necessity. It is an investment in trouble-free driving.

Know how to handle emergencies. The expert knows that he will come face to face with emergencies just when they're least expected. There's a theory that good drivers have no emergencies—that by careful "defensive driving" they never allow them to arise. There is a good deal of truth in this. The bad driver is always rushing into emergencies; the good driver isn't.

Yet even the most careful motorists quite often face crises. And you will too. The way you handle these critical situations will be the test of your skill. We all like to think that we can control emergencies by avoiding, for example, the car that suddenly "shoots in" from a side street or the car that stops without warning ahead of us. And in fact these are emergencies that the skilled driver can control. The most dangerous emergencies are once-in-a-lifetime situations. Even so, there is a way to meet them.

SOME UNEXPECTED EMERGENCIES

1. Heavy oil drums falling off a truck and rolling toward your front wheels at 60 mph.

2. A drunken driver careening toward you on your side of the road.

3. A heavy piece of contractor's machinery coming loose from its towbar and veering into your lane.

4. A deer jumping out of a field and landing on your windshield or a pheasant flying into the hood release catch, making the hood fly up. (This happened to a Michigan driver at 70 mph. He couldn't see ahead, but he survived without an accident.)

These are all perilous emergencies because they are unpredictable. And it takes real car handling to survive them. The Michigan driver fortunately was highly skilled. He was an industrial salesman who had spent half a lifetime on the road in every imaginable traffic circumstance. Instead of panicky braking and steering (which have killed other drivers in similar "hood-up" emergencies), he knew that he should not waste time trying to see ahead. So he steered to a safe stop while looking down at the yellow line alongside his door. "I had planned for years

Some Unexpected Emergencies

If cargo falls off truck ...

Car on wrong side of road ...

Hood flies open...

what I would do," he said. "I knew that my hood might come up some day. It has happened to other drivers."

The way to think ahead for once-in-a-lifetime emergencies is to practice the basic skills so that you won't even start to panic. This book covers three main topics: the fine points of car handling (Part One); sophisticated driving techniques (Part Two); and driving under dangerous conditions (Part Three). The expert driver, by mastering the skills described in these three sections, becomes one who avoids accidents while enjoying the road and his travels.

Good judgment is the password to expert driving. There are no absolutes.

It can never be said that any single driving technique is entirely safe. Everything you do when driving can be dangerous under some conditions.

Thus no one can really ever lay down driving rules or suggest useful techniques and say, "This is always the good way to do it. This is always the safe way."

All of the techniques and pointers mentioned in this book must be employed with greatest care and judgment, and always with due regard for "conditions" and safety. Some of them—especially the emergency procedures—definitely involve some risks. A man at a crash scene with a flashlight or flare, trying to save other motorists from disaster in the same pileup, is always in some danger and sometimes in very great danger.

There are times in some "tight" situations when even taking one hand off the wheel in order to activate a turn blinker, as required by law, is definitely dangerous. In this brief act a driver may lose the maximum steering control he needs to avoid a turn-collision. Even the simple act of lowering your headlights properly for other cars, as required by common sense and by law, sometimes creates hazards. There are times on the highway when slow speed is more dangerous than greater speed. Even using one's brakes involves constant risks—and has resulted in literally millions of rear-end collisions.

In short, you can get in trouble with any and all driving techniques. The true expert is the driver who knows the most advanced techniques. But he also uses good judgment—and determines the right and the wrong time to use them.

CHAPTER II

YOUR CAR'S DAILY "HEALTH CHECK"

DRIVING ISN'T ALL TIME SPENT behind the wheel. Pilots and boatmen know the importance of preparing for a journey. Motorists should prepare, too.

The "Bug Sheet." Preparation for your driving really should start when you put your car away at night. An airline pilot on finishing a flight fills out a "bug sheet." This is a list of all the things he found wrong with his plane that will need correction before the next flight. Similarly you should keep a notebook in your glove compartment to record after each trip what needs attention before you start again next morning. For example, the right-turn signal is not canceling or one door is not closing properly.

The Daily Car Check. Before starting each day's trip walk all the way around your car and examine the tires, lights (are any lenses broken?), and doors (closed tightly?).

Garage-Floor Inspection. Examine your garage floor for signs of trouble. Rusty water on the floor between the front wheels indicates a leaky cooling system, which could cause overheating on the highway and leave you stranded. Dark blue-black stains under the engine indicate oil leakage that could ruin your engine.

A puddle of pink, gray, or tan liquid under the front-seat position indicates that fluid is leaking from the automatic transmission. An expensive ($300–$500) transmission can be damaged if the fluid gets too low. Don't delay a single day in getting this corrected. A brown puddle that smells burned indicates not only that your transmission is leaking but that it has already been damaged inside.

The Garage Floor

FRONT OF CAR

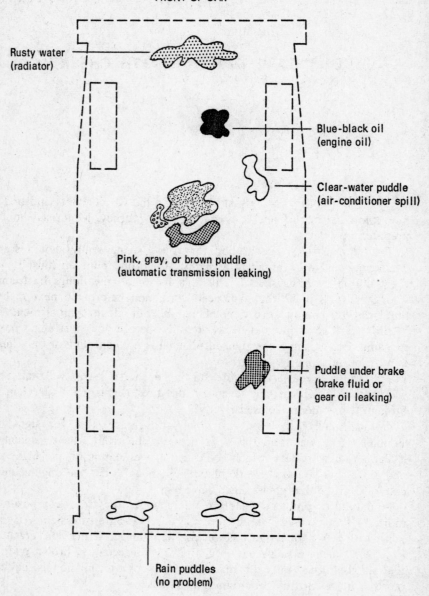

Rusty water
(radiator)

Blue-black oil
(engine oil)

Clear-water puddle
(air-conditioner spill)

Pink, gray, or brown puddle
(automatic transmission leaking)

Puddle under brake
(brake fluid or
gear oil leaking)

Rain puddles
(no problem)

Cloudy fluid trickling down the inner side of a tire could indicate that a brake line has rusted out near a wheel. Your brakes could be ready to fail. Immediate repairs are needed. Dark fluid on a rear tire means grease is leaking from the rear axle.

Do not confuse any of the above with puddles of normal water or melted snow that may drip from your car and are harmless. If your car has an air conditioner, do not be concerned if clear water drips (from one side of the engine compartment) when you turn your engine off on a hot day. This is normal.

CHAPTER III

STEERING POSITION AND THE FEEL

OF THE CAR

ONLY AFTER YOU HAVE COMPLETED the exterior daily check are you ready to get behind the wheel—but don't start the engine until you've gone through this additional checklist:

1. *Lock your doors.* This adds strength to your car's body in the event of a rollover. In tests made by a major automobile manufacturer many cars were run off a road and rolled over. Unlocked doors flew open and roofs and windshields were crushed. But locked doors stayed shut longer. They strengthened the roof, and they helped to keep it and the windshield frame from caving in (which means much less chance of injury to occupants).

2. *Adjust the seat height.* Always "sit tall." Look over the wheel, never through it. In some cars a driver who looks over the wheel can actually see the road fifty feet closer to his front wheels than a driver who looks through the wheel. If you are below average height and your seat has no vertical adjustment, sit on a large, firm cushion. Later we will look at other points about correct driving positions.

3. *Fasten your seat belt and shoulder harness,* preferably before you start the motor. (The only exception is when you have to back out of a driveway. See "The Best Backing Turn," page 14.)

THE IMPORTANCE OF SEAT BELTS

Seat belts are part of the good driver's correct driving position. Some drivers think the only reason for having seat belts is to keep people from being thrown through windshields. Actually in many accidents the major value of seat belts is their ability to keep people from being thrown through the doors.

However, belts have other practical advantages that have nothing to do with accidents. A belt firms you in the seat and actually makes steering easier on corners and curves.

Belts help prevent fatigue, on long trips especially. Consider just one example. On sharp right turns a surprising amount of your body weight is thrown against your left hand as it grips the wheel. And on a left turn the *right* hand gets the weight. But a seat belt by supporting your body eliminates much of this weight shifting.

Belts help in braking. In a panic-stop crisis a belt holds you back and keeps your full weight from being thrown on the brake through your braking foot. This allows you to apply and release brakes as necessary to avoid a skid.

After your belts are fastened, adjust your windshield and side rearview mirrors. A good driver always knows what's in back of him at all times and rearview mirrors are indispensable for this.

Once these preliminaries are taken care of, you can start your car.

GETTING STARTED

The Noisy Morning "Rev-Up." One way you can spot an inept driver is by the noise his engine makes during a cold-morning warm-up. The unskilled driver turns the starter key and revs up in a series of ear-shattering blasts. This blows out a good deal of oil and smoke and bothers the neighbors. It also hurts the engine.

A good driver starts his engine and lets it idle quietly, without noisy racing. His car moves out so quietly that the neighbors never hear it go.

Apart from bad manners, what is so wrong with the noisy rev-up? If you think of your car as an eager athlete waiting to get going, you have the answer. An athlete warms up slowly to get his system adjusted and his blood circulating before putting his body to the test. An engine needs warming up in exactly the same way—slowly. It too has a "system" that must warm up to the demands about to be put upon it. And it too has a bloodstream. This is the thin, steady flow of warm oil that must circulate rapidly through its arteries. When your engine is very cold, the oil is frigidly viscous and cannot circulate efficiently. Even thin "winter oils" thicken to a degree. All oil must be heated before it can flow— and lubricate—well. Revving up a cold engine before the oil is flowing easily puts a strain on sensitive inner metallic parts, for these were made to rub together only when well lubricated.

The Proper Warm-Up. Auto-company engineers advocate giving an engine a quiet one-minute driveway warm-up on very cold winter days. On warm days no warm-up is needed. But expressway driving is different.

Even on warm days it is unwise to run your car at expressway speeds before it is warmed up. A good driver works a cold engine up gradually from 40 to 55 mph. When temperatures hover near zero, your car may require many minutes of running at around-town speeds to heat your engine for high-speed or expressway driving. On such days you must also give thought to the other moving parts in your car that are bitterly cold: the fast-spinning wheels, the differential, and the transmission. These get no benefit of engine heat at all.

Your Steering Position. The first rule of good handling is to seat yourself firmly but comfortably at the controls. The well-handled car almost becomes an extension of your nervous and muscle systems. It is impossible to control an automobile well when you sit unsteadily or too stiffly, or when your feet have poor contact with the pedals and floor (as is sometimes the case with women who wear long, slender heels).

After settling your body solidly in the seat, be sure that your arms do not reach too high to steer. Drivers who keep both hands near the top of the wheel often get thrown to one side on sharp corners. This pulls the wheel around and makes it difficult to keep smooth control. Furthermore, if you sit too low, your hands actually block your view of the road.

Your body's weight should never be thrown on the steering wheel.

Keep your hands lightly but firmly on the wheel. Never cling to it and hang on for dear life, as you see some drivers do on turns. This robs you of all "precision control." It leaves you sadly off balance in case a sudden change of direction becomes necessary. For example, you start to make a sharp left turn. A dog runs out on the curve ahead of you. You have to jog suddenly to the right to miss it. A driver who is off balance may hit the dog or wreck the car.

And never be the driver who leans in the direction in which he's turning. This is the weakness of unstable drivers. Your head and torso should always remain upright. Only in this way can you make the sensitive judgments you need to control your car in expert fashion. Learn to feel and understand every movement and sound of your car. Note how long it takes to start turning after you spin the wheel. The more you develop this sense of "feel," the better you will drive.

CHAPTER IV

AROUND-TOWN CAR HANDLING

YOUR OWN FINESSE at car handling may be a topic of discussion—among friends—more often than you realize. And your neighbors' judgment is often quite accurate.

How, then, are you judged on your around-town car handling? In these basic ways:

1. *By Your Driving Smoothness.* Neighbors notice your starts, your turns, your speed going down the block, and whether you stop for stop signs. They also note whether your car lurches, sways on turns, suddenly changes direction, or makes abrupt lane changes. Does it tilt back when starting? Does it "hump" or "dive" forward when stopping? Do you force other drivers into evasive maneuvers: twists, turns, braking, or horn blowing?

2. *By Your Quietness.* It could almost be said of the expert: No one knows he is around. Neighbors rarely see—or hear—him come or go. His car is never spectacular in appearance or in action. It makes no noise when starting or stopping. The expert's tires don't squeal.

3. *By Your Ability to Put Passengers at Ease.* You've heard people say, "I'm afraid to drive with so-and-so." Or "He makes me nervous because he drives too close to the car ahead." Or "She takes chances." (You've also heard friends say, "She talks constantly while driving and never watches the road.")

Your driving finesse begins when you're backing out of the driveway. One maneuver that reveals an inept driver is backing at fast speed. Backing is one of the greatest causes of minor—and some major—accidents. Backing has probably smashed more rear fenders, quarter panels, bumpers, taillights, and deck hoods than any other maneuver drivers make. And backing kills or injures many small children in streets or driveways.

Not knowing this, the inept driver sometimes puts his car in reverse, kicks the gas pedal, and whirls out backward. This showy kind of driver is sharply increasing his chances of having an accident.

The expert knows that the fastest speed for backing is a slow crawl.

The Best Backing Turn. Your left hand is on the steering wheel at, say, the "two-o'clock" position. The right arm is stretched out along the back of the seat. You check your mirrors first, then turn your head to look back while moving in reverse. Your foot is ready to hit the brake.

(Special note for left-foot brakers: If you employ left-foot braking [see page 91], you will find that dragging the brake very lightly with the left foot whenever you drive backward is an excellent idea. It affords split-second stopping control if needed.)

And here's a trick that makes any backing turn quicker and neater. Many drivers turn their wheel one way only while backing. They (*a*) make a backing turn, (*b*) start forward, and (*c*) then turn their wheels the other way. This results in an awkward maneuver that requires extra space and effort. A better way is to (*a*) begin the backing turn, (*b*) turn the wheels the other way while still moving back and just before the backing maneuver ends, and (*c*) then start forward with wheels already turned the way you wish to go.

Avoid the reverse-to-forward lurch. Some drivers after backing hastily throw their automatic transmissions into forward drive and feed a little gas even before the car has finished moving backward. A sharp lurch results. This can damage the delicate clutches and brakes that are contained in an automatic transmission.

After using the reverse gear, make a full stop and pause for an instant before going into forward drive. Resist the temptation to start forward too soon.

Good Stopping. Stopping is just as important as driving, around town. Several characteristics distinguish the expert's ability to stop a car, especially at traffic lights:

1. His quiet stop.
2. The ample distance he leaves between his car and the one on his right or left.
3. The "elbow stop."

If a good driver arrives at a stop light and finds another car already waiting, he does not pull up "even bumpers" with the other car. He stops at the other driver's elbow. It's a sophisticated way of saying: "You were here first; you go first." Traffic lights present other situations that will demand the utmost of your driving skills.

If You Get Blocked in an Intersection. Suppose you enter an intersection on a green light but get "hung up" behind an obstruction such as a stalled car. You're caught in the middle of cross-traffic. When the light changes, cars press in toward you from both sides. Horns blow. What should you do? Try to proceed? Wait? Back up? Technically you still have right of way to complete the crossing. You may proceed when safe. Sometimes, however, it's not prudent to attempt to claim your right of way. But suppose drivers in back of you start blowing their horns angrily, trying to panic you into crossing?

The best thing is to stay where you are. But don't ignore those protesting drivers. Glance at them in a friendly way. Let them see that you are trying to find a way to clear the intersection. A friendly shrug, with hands lifted helplessly, usually quiets impatient drivers and informs them of your problem.

AVOIDING COLLISIONS

The Misunderstood Corner Collision. The corner on a slow-speed neighborhood block is a real trickster. Many people have been killed at such corners and at speeds as low as 10 mph. Don't underestimate this hazard. National Safety Council experts say "the corner nearest home"—the one a driver passes every day—is apt to be the place where he will someday have a collision.

In the main there are five kinds of corner collision against which every driver should be on guard:

1. *The Light-Change Collision.* You start when the light turns green. Just as you (*A*) get halfway across, you see *B* coming. Hidden by parked or moving cars, *B* has decided to run the light a second or two after it has changed. And because his foot is pushing hard on the gas, his car hits yours with great force.

The Light-Change Collision

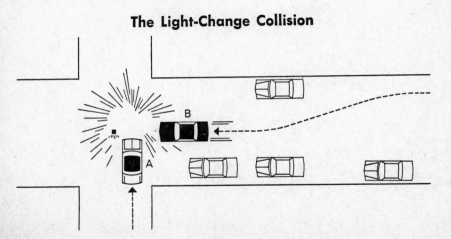

The Right-Side—Passer Collision

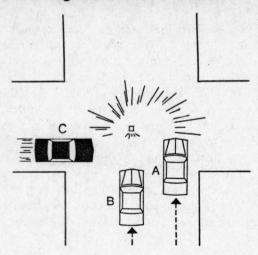

2. *The Right-Side—Passer Collision.* A pulls up for a red-light stop beside B. When B is slow in starting, A shoots impatiently ahead and fails to see why B was so slow to start. As a result, A gets hit by C— another last-minute traffic-light runner.

3. *The Blocked Left-Turn Collision.* A waits behind B. B starts, and his turn signal shows that he plans to turn left. A then starts. But just then B gets blocked by a pedestrian and has to stop short. Caught by surprise, A hits B.

The Blocked Left-Turn Collision

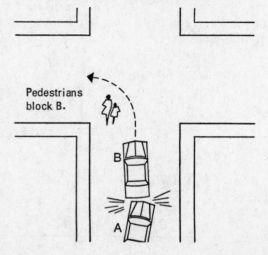

Pedestrians block B.

The Corner Tailgaiter

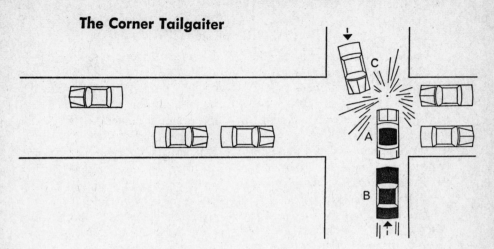

4. *The Corner Tailgater.* A starts fast. B starts fast. Suddenly C cuts across, trying to beat A. A stops and gets hit from behind by B.

5. *The Right-Turn Collision You Don't Think About.* One tricky street-corner hazard involves you (A) and the car parked at the end of the block, Z. Before making any right turn, always be sure that Z is not getting ready to start. Collisions sometimes happen when Z moves ahead just as A begins to turn.

The Right-Turn Collision You Don't Think About

BEWARE THE PEDESTRIAN

Pedestrians also tax the abilities of the expert driver. Here are some typically dangerous situations.

Pedestrians on Your Left. All drivers are properly taught: Watch for pedestrians who step out between parked cars on your right. Motorists are also taught to watch for people walking on the highways at night on the right!

But a special lookout should be kept at all times for the pedestrian who crosses unexpectedly *from your left*—often while running. A study of accidents reveals that a surprising number of adults and children are hit while crossing from left to right—especially in midblock.

The Left-Turn Pedestrian Surprise. Another pedestrian whom you should actually hunt for is one who is doing exactly what he should: He's crossing properly in the crosswalk, even has the green light in his favor. He's the pedestrian (see sketch) who starts to cross East-West Street on your left just as you turn from North-South Street.

Here is how he may look to you during such a turn, and this explains why he is in such danger.

You see, the trouble is he moves with you as you turn.

His speed and yours are so related that he may be hidden behind your left windshield post and may stay there until it's simply too late for you to avoid him.

On a rainy day he is even more of a surprise. If your side window and windshield edge are blurred, you may make the entire turn and never see the pedestrian at all until he steps in front of your left fender.

The Busy Corner. When approaching busy corners be sure to look underneath cars standing near crosswalks. This is where many pedestrians, baby carriages, or bicycles are first detected. Even if you do not see pedestrians' feet, you see their moving shadows and, on rainy days, their reflections.

The Hard-to-Square Right Turn. Cornering is a problem in city streets. Here are some tips on how to make the hardest ones easy. Many wide cars tend to dive toward the left front wheel in a fast, tight right turn. They don't turn so quickly as you want them to and this sometimes causes your left front fender to cross the center line of the street into which you are turning. You can make slow-speed "power turns" in small, narrow cars if you accelerate lightly into a quick, tight turn. It is not wise to attempt this in a car with a wider-than-average wheelbase. In a large car start a corner turn wide so that your rear wheels don't hit the curb. Go into the turn with brakes on. Release the brakes only

The Left-Turn Pedestrian Surprise

The Shortcut Left Turn

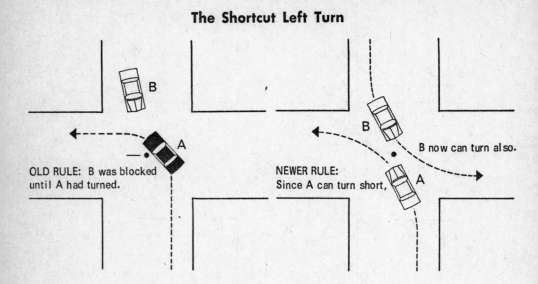

OLD RULE: B was blocked until A had turned.

NEWER RULE: Since A can turn short,

B now can turn also.

after turn is about 75 percent complete and you are sure that your left front fender won't hit opposing traffic. Now you can apply power to help complete the turn. This gives you a highly controlled turn without the unsettling dive toward the left front wheel.

The Shortcut Left Turn. Some communities still require you to pass the center of the intersection before turning left. Others wisely permit you to cut short, passing inside of the center point when practicable. This allows traffic to clear faster. However, it creates a hazard for pedestrians moving in the same direction as your car, so be careful.

Cutting inside the center point is almost always permitted, of course, if you are turning into a one-way street.

The Expert's "Clear-the-Track Turn." At some corners just one thoughtless driver waiting to turn can hold up a line of cars and deny them all a chance to move on the green light. When blocked in a left turn, the expert pulls well past the crosswalk if possible so that at least one or two cars can move up and turn left with him before the light turns red.

Turning in a Tight Spot. If you have to make a very tight turn—as in a narrow street or a parking garage—it's wise to use dead-slow speed. Your front wheels, in any fast turn, tend to slide (or "drift") sideways. Thus you need more room for turning.

The Thoughtless Corner Turner

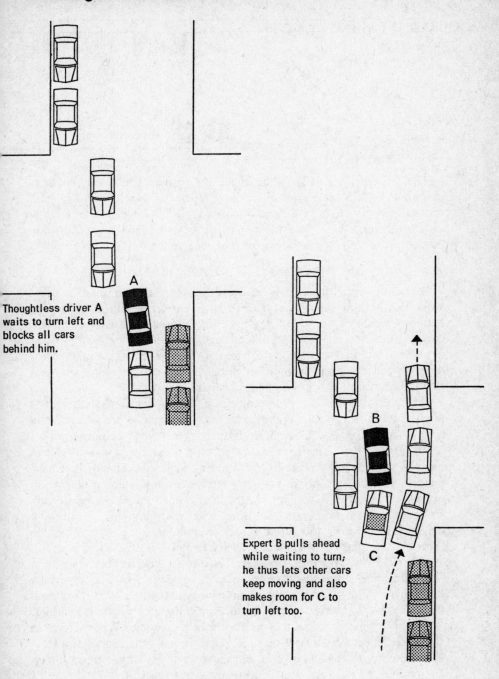

Thoughtless driver **A** waits to turn left and blocks all cars behind him.

Expert **B** pulls ahead while waiting to turn; he thus lets other cars keep moving and also makes room for **C** to turn left too.

Quicker U-Turns

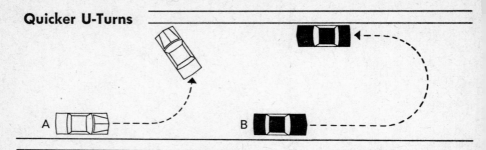

This is important, too, when making U-turns. These can be dangerous, so get them over very quickly. How? By turning slowly! Fast turning may cause you to hit the opposite curb, back up, and then come forward again. But a U-turn made at dead-slow speed takes less time because it usually can be completed in one maneuver.

BRAKING: GOOD AND BAD

An inept driver's brake light is forever flashing, showing that he overworks his brakes. This is because he is an uneven driver, speeding up and slowing down too often. A good driver's brake lights rarely go on, except when he definitely sees danger ahead or is making a stop, as at a traffic light. In fact, a good driver may go two hundred miles on a limited-access highway without touching his brakes. He will spend less than other drivers for tires and brake repairs.

When you have to use your brakes, use "early-warning" flashes. It is good practice to tap your brake pedal once or twice before you actually have to apply brakes. These early flashes warn drivers behind you.

The Panic Stop. All drivers now and then get caught by surprise and have to "lock" their brakes to avoid hitting a bumper ahead. If it happens to you on rare occasions—say once a year—you're probably an average driver. But if you get caught in two such "panic stops" in any six-month period, something is wrong with your driving. You may be driving too close or too fast for road conditions; or you may not be "reading the road" as you should. (See Chapter XI.)

Don't Be an "Accordion Maker." No doubt you've been caught in some tiresome stop-and-go jams on overcrowded highways, especially on holidays. For several moments all cars are stopped. Next, they rush pell-mell ahead. Then they stop again (and bumpers sometimes get hit).

Traffic engineers know this as "accordion" trouble. When there's a slowdown ahead, don't rush up to it, then jam on your brakes and stop. Instead, cut your speed *early* so that last-minute braking is unnecessary. Time your speed so the jam will break as you reach it.

Left-Foot Braking. For the advanced driver who drives a car with automatic transmission, left-foot braking offers tremendous advantages. (See Chapter XVI.) It gives split-second control if a child runs out or a pedestrian steps hurriedly off the curb. Your left foot is already applying the brake even before your right foot can be lifted off the gas.

When moving through any congested street, especially in a narrow traffic lane, it sometimes pays to drag the left foot on the brake very lightly. This, of course, puts extra wear on the brakes, but it also adds an extraordinary degree of control when maneuvering under risky conditions. Danger of accident is greatly reduced. Don't overdo it, however. Don't let your left foot get into the lazy habit of resting on the brake pedal at all times—as some drivers do. This quickly wears out brake linings.

Downshift Braking: Avoid It. Some drivers whose cars are equipped with standard transmission like to shift from third to second gear or—on some cars—from fourth to third to second on approaching sharp corners.

This throws heavy wear on transmissions. It is all right, however, to use second gear (on all standard-transmission cars) to help your brakes hold the car back on very steep mountain highways. Downshifting is also a good emergency slowing device in case your brakes should ever fail. (See "How to Stop a Runaway Car," page 148.) On some automatic-transmission cars the second range has considerable braking power for emergency use, but on others it has very little.

SPECIAL POINTERS ON PARKING

Everyone knows the standard way of curb parking: pull up abreast of the car at the curb (*A*) until rear bumpers are even, then back slowly and cut the wheel sharply until your driving seat is aligned with *A*'s left taillight. Your car should now be at a forty-five-degree angle. Next, straighten wheels, then back in at a forty-five-degree angle. As tire approaches curb, reverse wheel—sharply—and now back in very slowly.

Parking

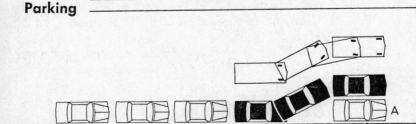

All this works well if car *A* is neatly parked close to the curb, is not parked at an angle, and happens to be a car of similar size and shape to yours.

But what do you do when car *A* is much wider or much smaller than yours? Or when *A* is parked, as it often is, with rear wheel three feet from the curb?

Here are some suggestions that make parallel parking easier:

1. *Do it with mirrors.* Many drivers have parking trouble because they are not able to judge, while moving backward, where their rear bumpers are. One trick is to watch your car's reflection in a store window. This reveals where the rear of your car is going. It shows the bumper of the car behind you. And it may even show how close your rear wheel is to the curbstone. What's more, the mirror shows clearly if pedestrians try to walk behind you.

2. *Look for "open end" parking.* Some drivers try to crowd into difficult parking spots when there are easier places only a few car lengths away. Look for a place at either end of the block where there will be no car in front or no car behind you.

3. *Know where your wheel well is.* To gain confidence in parking, it pays to know exactly where the wheel well is. This is the rounded metal hump (often visible beside the rear seat) that covers each rear wheel.

To fix this position in mind, sit at the steering wheel, give a friend a yardstick, and ask him to stand outside the car by your right rear wheel. Have him hold the yardstick in a vertical position close to the wheel hub. Now, by glancing over your right shoulder you can see the yardstick through the window and get a better idea of where your wheel is at all times.

4. *Measure the overhang.* The overhang is the troublesome rear section of your car behind the rear wheels that makes parking difficult. It hides both the curb and the bumper of the car behind you.

Use a yardstick and measure the distance from rear wheel to rear bumper.

Once you know the distance, ask a friend to stand behind your car and hold the yardstick vertically above the center of your rear bumper so you can see it. Repeat at left and right ends of the bumper until you have a firm idea of where that important—but hidden—piece of your car really is! This can be especially helpful to drivers who have to operate a car longer than the one they are used to.

CHAPTER V

A LOOK AT SPEED: CONFUSING CONFLICTS

WHEN THIS NEW REVISION of *Expert Driving* was in preparation, it was originally planned that the following chapter would be rewritten, dropping mention of speeds above 55-mph which Congress now has declared illegal.

But after careful consideration of some troublesome facts (outlined on page 36) we felt it was important to present the chapter as *originally written* (when speed limits of 60 and 70 were common), with only minor changes.

Despite recent developments (and the constantly changing enforcement picture), it was felt that the chapter contains valuable background facts which every driver must understand in order to gain good judgment and a sound understanding of problems that come with speed.

And so you will find some reference to real-life problems now encountered by some drivers, legally and illegally, at speeds below and above 55. To obscure these would be to put blinders on the reader and deny the full perspective needed. For there are times when many law-respecting drivers *are* tempted to "bend" the law; and times when some may be actually forced to—*by police inability to enforce the speed law uniformly.* (An example would be when a driver is chased downhill by two trucks which are running side-by-side and trying to accelerate to 70 in order to make the *next* hill.)

This, then, must be regarded by the reader mainly as a "consciousness-raising" chapter. And the following hard-nosed facts must be remembered:

1. Except as a few states may undertake to change it locally, the law of the land *is* 55 mph.

2. Exceeding 55 *is* a violation.

3. Good drivers do not willfully violate the law. (In fact, most actually *want* to see it enforced fairly and uniformly.)

4. To have an accident above the speed limit may seriously hurt your chances of insurance recovery—a major point to be remembered!

Every car has its own best speed. Any driver can determine by a little careful observation and feel what speed his car "likes best." This is the speed at which the car runs quietly, feels very stable, handles easily, and responds instantly to all maneuvers, without sudden weight shifts, tire squealing, or discomfort.

Some cars, given the right sort of highway (and ideal traffic conditions), run quite well hour after hour at 65–70. Others, usually older cars, can't stand a steady pace over 60. They become noisy and hard to handle.

All passengers, too, have their own best speed. Passengers know instinctively when a car is exceeding its own best "natural" speed. They sense, too, when a driver is going faster than his own experience and ability warrant. They are comfortable with the calm, confident driver and uneasy with the inept, inexperienced driver who goes from blunder to scary blunder.

And the considerate driver is aware of all this. If his passengers squirm, become alarmed, or try to push imaginary brake pedals through the floorboard, he slows down.

A driver should remember at all times: He feels a sense of security that the passenger cannot possibly have. After all, the driver has a steering wheel to hold, but the passenger has none. Even if the steering wheel offers little real protection to the driver, it nevertheless gives him a psychological shield. He has control of it. He knows where he can make the car go.

In addition, he has both the accelerator and brake pedal under his control.

But the poor passenger, especially the one in the right front seat, has none of this security. He feels himself hurled down the road into situations not of his own making. He's a captive.

"Speed kills": True or False? What are the facts? The trouble with slogans and catch phrases is their brevity. Brevity makes slogans attractive to use and easy to pass on to others.

"Speed kills," then, is sometimes true, sometimes false—depending on what you mean by "speed" and on the conditions under which it is employed. A car that is traveling at 35 mph on a busy expressway in rush hour, for example, may well be twice as dangerous as one going a legal 50.

Whether speed kills, then, depends on several things:

How much speed is meant? 35 mph in a 60-mph zone? An illegal 80 mph in a 50-mph zone?

How fast is everyone else going? Very often it is difference in speed that counts.

How straight and wide (or how crooked and narrow) is the road?
How good is the car? The tires?
How experienced is the driver?
Has the driver had a drink? Is he tired?
How good is the weather? Is the road wet? Icy? Dry?
How smooth is the roadway? Surface bumpy? (A car going over "washboard" bumps at even 45 mph may lose half its traction because its tires are bouncing and not touching the road all the time.)

WHAT THE NATIONAL SAFETY COUNCIL SAYS

Statisticians of the National Safety Council, after studying many accident reports, have come up with these interesting facts:

If a driver is going 75 mph and an accident happens, he is fairly likely to die or be very badly hurt. The chances that he will be killed, in fact, are one in eight. That's pretty high. And the accident need be nothing more than a tire blowout.

If he is going 65 mph when the accident happens, he improves his hope of survival considerably. Now the chances of death are one in twenty. This is still quite high.

But if he is traveling at a rate of only 55 mph when a crash happens, he improves his chances tremendously. Now there is only one chance in fifty that he will die.

Who are those "good fast drivers"—and are they safer?

The faster drivers who do seem to have excellent, accident-free records are certainly not the town showoffs who drive down the main street or past the schoolhouse at 70 mph.

The faster drivers should be called "smooth" rather than "fast." The brisk, "smooth" driver keeps moving but rarely gets arrested because he is not a speeder and does not bother other drivers. He makes no dramatic starts and stops. He does not cut in and out. He makes fast time mainly because he keeps a steady, smooth pace and constantly watches the road ahead. (See Chapter XI.)

While other drivers get trapped and delayed in little jams, he usually manages to keep moving because he is quick to see when jams are forming.

An interesting fact about smooth drivers is this: They often reach their destination ahead of the speeders although they don't go so fast. This happens because the speeder is in many ways a poor driver. In his haste to get ahead at all costs he switches from lane to lane, rushes up behind slow trucks or cars, and often gets "boxed in." On a hundred-mile trip he may overtake the same smooth driver several times in great bursts of speed. Yet the smooth driver keeps forging ahead. He does this simply by moving ahead at a steady, unspectacular rate, avoiding the little jams that delay the less skilled speeder.

HOW OFFICIALS DECIDE ON SAFE SPEED LIMITS

Every driver should know how safe speed limits are determined by the officials whose job it is to erect speed-limit signs.

When a highway is to be "signed" for speed, speed-recording radar units are set up beside the road and everyone's speed is measured. Officials determine the speed at which eighty-five percent of all drivers are moving, and this becomes the official limit for that particular stretch of road.

This is known as the "eighty-five percentile" system of finding safe speed limits. The significant point is this: Officials have found that most drivers are wise in judging the best speed for any given set of conditions. If, when in doubt, you use the speed that most other drivers are using, you are probably close to the best speed for that particular stretch of road.

WHAT YOU SHOULD KNOW ABOUT "SPEED HYSTERIA"

State police in Connecticut have made an interesting discovery: On certain days a kind of "speed hysteria" seems to infect drivers.

Usually these are bright, clear days when the wind is from the northwest, and the air is crisp and bracing. "On such days," Connecticut troopers say, "some drivers seem to go a little faster than usual. Then speed becomes contagious and soon nearly everybody seems to be going too fast."

Speed hysteria is often evident on crowded city expressways during the rush hour, especially when drivers are homeward bound at the end of the day. Suddenly everyone is driving pell-mell. This is rush-hour commuter traffic, perhaps the fastest mass-traffic flow in the world. And this is a time when the uneasy driver who has had little experience should stay away from expressways.

HOW SPEEDOMETERS CAN CAUSE TROUBLE

Speedometers often give an inaccurate report on car speed. Some are too fast; others are too slow. A fast-reading speedometer might, for example, indicate a speed of 63 mph although the car may be going only 60 mph. A slow-reading speedometer might read 55 mph when a car is going 60 mph.

However, an inaccurate speedometer is not accepted as a legal excuse for driving too fast (or too slow).

Every driver should test his own speedometer now and then. Furthermore, it is well to test its rate of error (if it has any) at different speeds. Tests have shown that a speedometer which reads too fast at 45 mph might read too slow at 70 mph.

To test your speedometer, watch for signs reading "TEST MILE AHEAD," or "FIVE-MILE TEST RANGE." The longer ranges give you more accurate readings. Have your passenger watch the second hand of his wristwatch. Decide in advance which of your speedometer readings you wish to test first. Suppose it is to be the 50-mph reading. Set your speed so that the speedometer indicates an even 50 before you come to the "BEGIN TEST" sign. Now hold the speed as even as possible. Since it will be virtually impossible to hold the needle exactly on the 50 mark for very long, compensate for your own errors. If you see that your speed rises to 52, compensate by lowering speed for approximately the same interval of time to 48 mph.

As you pass the "BEGIN TEST" sign, call, "Mark!" to your time-keeper. He should note the position of the second hand on his watch. At the last sign, call, "Mark!" again. Now your passenger notes how many minutes and/or seconds elapsed during the run.

At 50 mph you should run a one-mile test (see table below) in exactly seventy-two seconds (one minute and twelve seconds). If your elapsed time was three seconds more, then your speedometer is reading too fast. Your true speed was only 48 mph. If your time was three seconds less than seventy-two seconds, however, your true speed was approximately 52.2 mph. Your speedometer is reading two miles an hour too slow.

If 1-mile test takes . . .	If 3-mile test takes . . .	If 5-mile test takes . . .	Car's true speed is . . .
120 secs.	6 mins. (360 secs.)	10 mins. (600 secs.)	30 mph
90 secs.	4 mins. 30 secs.	7½ mins. (450 secs.)	40 mph
72 secs.	3 mins. 36 secs.	6 mins. (360 secs.)	50 mph
60 secs.	3 mins. (180 secs.)	5 mins. (300 secs.)	60 mph
51.4 secs.	2 mins. 34 secs.	4 mins. 17 secs.	70 mph
48 secs.	2 mins. 24 secs.	4 mins. (240 secs.)	75 mph
45 secs.	2 mins. 15 secs.	3 mins. 45 secs.	80 mph

WHY DO SPEEDOMETERS GIVE WRONG READINGS?

On some older cars speedometer error was "built in." That is, speedometers were built to show a slightly higher speed than cars actually traveled. This was supposed to be a safety measure. It also made drivers think they were going faster. Today the general practice is to equip cars with accurate speedometers, but even modern speedometers suffer from wear.

HOW TO PREVENT SPEEDOMETER FAILURE

If the recording needle begins to quiver slightly or jump back and forth erratically, have the speedometer cable checked immediately. Usually cable lubrication is all that is needed.

Your tires, of course, also affect your "true" speed. Suppose that you have an accurate speedometer and that when you go 60 mph, it reads exactly 60. But then winter arrives. You start down a road. The speedometer says 60 mph—the exact speed limit. But suddenly a man with a badge is handing you a speeding ticket.

The fault may be with the snow tires that you installed yesterday. Snow tires, larger in diameter than ordinary tires, make your car go several miles an hour faster than the speedometer shows. You thought you were going 60 mph, but your big new tires were pushing you along at 63 or 64.

DO POLICE REALLY ALLOW "SPEED TOLERANCE"?

No doubt you have heard, as many drivers have, that the police will really let you drive slightly faster than the posted speed limit. In other words (or so you've been told) you may not get a ticket in a 55-mph zone until you're going 60.

Here is the fact. It is generally recognized today that speed-law enforcement must be slightly flexible. This is because road conditions keep changing from hour to hour. As an example, some fine, wide roads in shopping areas have to be posted at 40 mph because it would be unsafe to go faster during rush hours when many shoppers are afoot. And yet at 11:00 P.M., after all stores are closed, these roads are wide and empty and drivers naturally chafe at having to go only 40 mph. At such times unreasonably slow speed limits breed disrespect for law. Under such conditions police may know that 45 mph is quite safe and the truth is that they often permit it.

On the open highway, too, police do sometimes allow "tolerance." But tolerance always depends on two things: the condition of the road and the way in which each driver is handling his car. Suppose the speed limit is 55 mph. Traffic is light. A smooth, even driver who is not changing lanes and is not bothering other drivers might be permitted to drive 60 mph. But another driver, who is cutting in and out or accelerating noisily, might be arrested for driving 57 mph, only two miles over the posted limit.

In some states police rely on the speed law as a weapon to use when necessary against the driver who is obviously driving in an improper manner.

But don't count on speed tolerance. Not all police departments have the same point of view. Some still adhere to the older policy: If anyone goes one mile an hour over the speed limit, he's a lawbreaker. Arrest him! This is still true in a few "speed-trap" towns.

And a policy of strict enforcement still prevails on highways on which accidents are numerous. If several people get hurt on several successive weekends on any given stretch of highway, the police may suddenly abandon any policy of tolerance that they might have had.

HOW FAST SHOULD YOU GO?

It isn't easy to define safe speed, for "speed" has a different meaning every moment of the day. And it means different things to different drivers.

THESE ARE THE FACTS

Speed Fact No. 1: Speed under proper control may not necessarily cause accidents, but if an accident does occur, it does increase risk. There's no question about this. If a badly driven car leaves the road at 45 mph, it may get back. But at 60 it's in real trouble.

Speed Fact No. 2: The faster a car goes, the better the driver must be. A car at 40 mph is quite manageable for a beginner, and it's wise for beginners to stick to 40-mph roads. The super-roads—especially busy city expressways—are strictly for more experienced drivers.

Speed Fact No. 3: It is relative speed that really counts. Your speed in relation to the speed of other cars on the road is as important as your speed in miles per hour. If you are going so fast that you are passing all other cars, you're in danger—for every additional pass you make is an additional hazard.

If you're traveling so slowly that many faster cars are passing you, you're in danger too—for the same reason. You're causing too many passing situations.

You're in least danger when all cars are traveling at nearly the same speed and are widely spaced. Some day all cars in certain lanes may be required to go at the same rate of speed. Until that day comes, your best rule is to move along smoothly with the traffic.

Speed Fact No. 4: In general the faster roads are the safer roads today because they present fewer obstacles. Accident records show that they are at least three times safer, as a rule, than the narrow old 50-mph highways.

Speed Fact No. 5: Speed should be changed frequently as conditions change.

WHAT IS YOUR BEST CRUISING SPEED?

The following table is not exact. It is an interesting exercise and it shows how you can determine your own best "trip cruising speed" by evaluating your car, the road, your passenger and baggage load, your trip weather, and yourself.

The table below was prepared by the author with the help of Chief Traffic Engineer William L. Carson, of the American Automobile Association, and Professor William J. Toth, of the New York University Safety Center, for publication in *Parade* magazine. It is based on conditions that prevail generally on super-highways.

It first takes into account four basic safety and comfort considerations. Then to these it adds ten "trip variables"—elements that change from trip to trip.

To apply it to your own driving, ask yourself the questions and score yourself once in each of the 14 categories:

1. How old is your car?	Comment	Score (check one)
Class A: New to 2 years.	New cars handle better in emergencies. For a Class	5 ☐
Class B: 2—4 years, good condition.	A car you'll find top permitted legal speed comfortable for passengers on	4 ☐
Class C: 4 years or older.	a super-road under ideal conditions: light traffic, dry road, skilled driver. Hold Class C cars five miles slower, at least.	3 ☐

2. How are the tires?

New or nearly new.	Speeds over 60 are unsafe for any but the best tires.	5 □
Some wear showing.	Don't drive recaps at sustained speeds over 55.	4 □
Much wear.	Hold well-worn tires to 45—and don't risk over 35	3 □
Recaps.	on bald treads. (Even *one* bald tire is very danger-	2 □
Treads worn bald.	ous—and illegal.)	0 □

3. How experienced is the driver?

Class A: Over 5 years experience, including much fast-highway driving.	Only Class A drivers should attempt to drive passengers at top legal speeds. Class E drivers are wise to hold top speed	5 □
Class B: Over 5 years but little time on fast highways.	to 50, Class D to 53.	4 □
Class C: 2–4 years.		3 □
Class D: 1–2 years.		2 □
Class E: 1 year or less.		1 □

4. How heavy will your load be?

Class A: Driver traveling alone.	Heavy-laden cars tend to sway at higher speed, are harder to stop in emergen-	5 □
Class B: 2 adults and luggage.	cies. If you're in Class C or D, hold top speed to 55. In Class E, don't go over	4 □
Class C: 3 adults, or 2 adults and 2 children with luggage.	50.	3 □
Class D: 4 adults, or 3 adults and 2 children with luggage.		2 □
Class E: Car tends to tip backward when fully loaded.		1 □

Total the four items above for your base speed score. (If, for example, you checked the first item under each question, your base speed now is 20.)

Base speed score: _____

Next, check the following "trip variables":

5. What kind of road will you use?

Superhighway.	4 ☐
Old-style 4-lane dual with intersections and driveways.	3 ☐
Old-style 2-way road.	1 ☐

6. What is the weather?

Clear.	Emergency rule of thumb: in heavy rainstorm, hold top speed to 42; less in gusty winds.	4 ☐
Light rain.		3 ☐
Heavy rain and wind.		1 ☐

7. How heavy is traffic?

Light (fewer than 7 cars in view in ¼-mile ahead).	4 ☐
Medium (10 cars in view in ¼-mile ahead).	3 ☐
Heavy (many cars moving smoothly).	2 ☐
Heavy and turbulent (bunchy, with many cars changing lanes).	1 ☐

8. Do your passengers mind speed?

No.	Nobody gets tense.	4 ☐
Yes.	Some get tense at higher speeds or in heavy traffic.	3 ☐

9. Will you face morning or afternoon sun glare?

No.	Glare is far more dangerous than has been recognized.	4 ☐
Yes.	It blinds you without your realizing it. In severe glare, cut speed at once by at least 10–15 mph.	3 ☐

10. Day or night trip?

Day.	In general when night falls your speed should drop at	4	☐
Night.	least 5 mph. Another point: You're overdriving your headlights at speeds over 50 mph.	1	☐

11. How comfortable is the weather?

Pleasant.	Everyone expects to feel fine.	4	☐
Hot and muggy.	Passengers will be uncomfortable, edgy, anxious to get it over with.	3	☐

12. Tired or fresh driver?

Driver will be behind wheel 1 to 5 hours in any day.   4 ☐

Over 5 hours.   3 ☐

13. How fresh is the driver?

He feels fine, no fatigue.   4 ☐

He is tired after a hard day's work or a poor night's sleep.   3 ☐

14. How well do you know the roads you'll use?

Know them well.   4 ☐

Unfamiliar with them.   3 ☐

Total variables_____

Add your base speed score_____

Total score_____

WHAT YOUR SCORE MEANS

You now have your "theoretical good-judgment cruise speed." For example, suppose you plan a three-hour trip in a newish car (5 points) with good tires (5 points). You have had years of fast-highway driving (5 points) and you will have one passenger (4 points.)

To these 19 points you then add the variables: super-highway, clear weather, heavy smooth traffic, nervous passenger, day trip (no glare), hot and muggy day; but you feel fine and know the road.

You'll "score" a 55-mile speed. This is merely an indicator that you *qualify* for 55. Adjust it properly as conditions vary!

But you return the following night in heavy traffic and rain, with two nervous passengers and you're tired. Now your "good-judgment speed" is 48.

THE TROUBLESOME SPEED FACTS

Any discussion of speed is complicated by these conflicts:

1. Our Inter-states were designed for 70, some even for 80, mph.

2. Many cars are powered to travel easily at 80.

3. But years of crumbling roads, starting in the 1970s, began to make such speeds unsafe.

4. Congress sprang a surprise when, to save fuel, it decided to lower the national limit (formerly 60, 70, 75, 80) to 55 mph. Then the new limit itself produced surprises: Many people liked it, and it began to save lives.

5. However, the "meaning" of a 55 mph limit began to be interpreted differently by different police (and by governors who oversee law enforcement).

6. Some police were reluctant to apply a 55 mph limit to big trucks.

7. Some police see the 55 mph limit as merely a "limiting device"— to discourage motorists who used to rush in and out of traffic at 70 and 80. (In this, it has been very successful. In most places there are far fewer "big speeders" today.)

8. Other police consider 55 to mean "the upper 50s" and don't issue tickets under 59 mph if drivers are seen to be careful.

9. However, even these "liberal" police see it as a needed weapon, ready to nab the intoxicated or erratic driver if he even ventures to 56 mph.

10. And, of course, some police enforce it strictly as written: 55 mph.

It is manifestly impossible to discuss speed definitively in terms of all these variables. This is why this chapter ranges over such a wide area of speeds and conditions. The two definitive facts which do emerge from the confusing situation are these: *The law as written by Congress lowered the limit to 55*; and as speed rises past this point the dangers and difficulties rise at an even steeper, disproportionate rate.

CHAPTER VI

STEERING: PRECISION CONTROL

ALL DRIVERS GET TIRED of steering on long trips. If you don't think this is true, watch other drivers closely on your next trip—and study your own steering methods.

On long trips drivers may start out in the morning sitting erect at the wheel in the best driving-school manner, with both hands properly on the wheel. But after an hour or two they begin to slouch a bit. By mid-afternoon you will see many different examples of steering "form." Many drivers who began the day with left hand comfortably at the nine-o'clock position on the wheel and right hand at the three- or four-o'clock position now have abandoned all form. They're getting tired. You will see many who appear to be driving with only one hand—usually the right hand in different positions, even at the bottom of the wheel.

HOW TO AVOID STEERING FATIGUE

The best cure for steering fatigue is probably the so-called tilt wheel, which can be raised or lowered into several different positions during the course of a trip. This wheel can be dropped so low that it almost touches the lap, in which position a tired driver's hands rest upon it lightly. He is spared all the effort that is usually needed to keep both hands elevated to the wheel. In short, he almost drives with his hands in his lap—a tremendous saving of energy and quite safe too.

However, tilt wheels are not available on all cars and, when available, cost extra dollars that many owners may not want to spend.

How else then can you avoid steering fatigue on long trips?

Slip Steering. One method used by many experienced drivers is slip steering. The right hand, at the two-, three- or four-o'clock positions,

37

does most of the work—at least on straight, easy stretches of road. The left hand, when not actually needed to help in turning, mainly acts as a kind of brake or clutch. It remains generally at the eight-o'clock position and as the wheel is turned, it merely grips the rim to help control it momentarily or else relaxes and lets the rim slip through the loosely clenched fist.

Besides being restful, this kind of steering, if done properly, has a second advantage: it steadies the driver. A driver clinging to a wheel with both hands in a series of turns now and then finds himself thrown from side to side by the movement of the car. This in turn forces him to throw some of his weight on the wheel and makes good steering difficult. If a sudden crisis happens in a tight, fast turn, he is caught off balance and is not able to meet it smoothly.

But the slip-steering driver feels no such instability. One reason for this is that he often uses another device:

Elbow-Contact Driving. There is no substitute for alertness and correct form in driving as taught in good driving classes. Nevertheless, you will notice that on long trips many advanced drivers—drivers of long experience—sit slightly to the left of center, with left elbow touching an armrest or with left knee touching the door. Some tall drivers rest their left arm against the window.

This might be termed "elbow-contact" driving or "knee-contact" driving. When done properly, it adds solid side-of-body contact with the car. It is employed by many advanced drivers at times. You will even see many veteran state troopers drive this way and they are, as a group, among the world's finest drivers. It has three advantages:

1. It often helps to improve your "feel" of the car, especially on bumpy roads, because you have added contact with the car.

2. It offers a comfortable change of position and helps combat fatigue on long trips.

3. It often stabilizes the driver.

But note this: The expert never leans his weight against his door. And his left arm never protrudes from an open window.

To judge the value of elbow-contact driving, try touching your elbow lightly to the armrest * briefly next time you make a sharp (say, 40 mph) right turn on a narrow, bumpy road. See how it adds to your feeling of control and stability. It gives you great precision control.

In short, elbow-control steering gives the expert (*a*) steadiness on curves and (*b*) a quicker sense of what the car is trying to do.

---

* If your car has no armrest on the driver's side, you can have one installed to fit you.

Slouchy Driving. Elbow-contact driving as done by experts on long trips is certainly not to be confused with slouchy driving. We all know the driver who lounges lazily far over to the left in a sloppy-looking car and rests his weight against the door. Often he steers with right hand alone, at the eleven-o'clock position. His left arm is outside the window and his left hand clutches the edge of the roof. His elbow is well outside the windowsill. (Many such drivers have lost their left arms in collisions.) He is usually a poor driver, prone to accidents (as the dents in his car attest). He is in danger of falling out or losing control if his door comes open. And he is in no position to make quick steering or braking adjustments in an emergency.

YOUR CAR'S "MESSAGE"

In all driving it is important to receive the dozens of "messages" that a car sends every minute—messages about direction, vibration, balance, tire grip, curve safety. Elbow-contact steering helps the experienced driver feel and receive this vital information because he is in such close personal touch with his car.

Getting these messages is vital because your car is forever shifting balance. And each small change in balance causes a change in direction. If you hadn't noticed this, try counting how many times you have to make slight steering adjustments with your hands in a single mile of perfectly straight road. Every uneven spot in the pavement requires a steering change. It is a rare car whose driver can keep his hands from moving at least once every three seconds.

The good driver will get some of these messages by sound, some by sight, but most by feel. This is why the expert settles himself so solidly and attentively at the wheel. In every possible way he is seeking precision control.

PRECISION CONTROL: WHAT IT IS

Some people who try to walk fast through a crowd seem to bump into everybody. They lack precision control. Others never bump into anybody. They have it.

As a good driver you will learn to do some extremely fine control work. Consider this example. You are approaching a sharp and difficult curve. Your car's speed is 45 mph. Then just as you enter the curve you see a bump or a chuckhole that could upset your timing, bounce your car, perhaps even throw your wheels off the road. An inept driver lacking full identity with his car will hit the bump and make a pretty bad turn of it. The skilled driver will actually turn one foot sooner, miss the bump by inches, and complete a flawless turn. Now, if you will take the time to figure this out, you will see that the one-foot timing difference between the good driver's turn and the bad driver's turn is very small indeed. It may be as little as one sixty-sixth of a second. (That's the time it takes your car to go one foot at 45 mph.)

On a long trip a good driver makes such fraction-of-a-second adjustments a thousand times a day. Yet it is plain that a driver who does not learn to become really part of his car while steering cannot hope to have precision control.

GET THE "FEEL" OF A STRANGE CAR

All cars have a slightly different response. It varies with make and model, age, load, kind of tires, condition of steering gear, condition of shock absorbers and other items. A driver who takes the wheel of an unfamiliar car and immediately proceeds to drive it in fast traffic may discover that the car will not do the things he expects if a slight emergency develops.

Because of this, experts make a special effort to feel out a strange car's responsiveness—good or bad—as soon as they start to drive. In the first few miles an expert will determine:

Brake response: Is it fast or slow?

How much unsettling "nose dive" is there in a sudden stop? A car that dives forward excessively may not handle with needed stability in a crisis.

How quick and solid is the steering response? Does the car steer instantly or is it slow to maneuver ("understeer") when the wheel is turned? Or, if it responds instantly, does it swerve too quickly ("oversteer") when the wheel is turned?

One way to learn the "feel" of a car is to test it carefully on a safe, deserted street or road. Set a slow speed (20–25 mph is fast enough). Now "waggle" the car a little from side to side. Pull the wheel right and left in small, quick maneuvers so that the car veers back and forth slightly (a foot or two) in its own lane. Then, during one mild veer, apply brakes. How does the car respond to all this? Does it feel secure or insecure? Does it sway from side to side? Or does it transmit a good, solid feel? Is there play in the steering gear? Do the brakes take hold smoothly and evenly without "pull" to either side even in a turn? A single waggle test like this will also tell whether the tires contain enough air. Under-inflated tires will give the car a sluggish, "squashy" feel, and such a car can be hard to control in a crisis.

CHAPTER VII

THE TRUTH ABOUT FOLLOWING DISTANCES

AN OLD RULE OF THUMB SAYS: "Stay one car length back for every 10 miles of speed."

This rule is easy to remember. But because of rising speed limits it has been discarded by some experts. In its place has come a new rule: "Stay two car lengths back for every 10 miles of speed."

There is merit in both rules and times when both are deficient.

How far back under today's traffic conditions should a driver really stay at:

35 mph on a downtown business street?

45 mph on an edge-of-town street lined with stores, gas stations, restaurants?

55 mph on a jammed city expressway?

One reason for rules varying is the blindgating accident. Here is how a blindgating accident happens:

At 55 mph driver *A*, observing the old "one car length" rule, is following six car lengths behind driver *B*. Or he may even be observing the "two car length" rule. It doesn't matter in dense traffic at 55 mph.

Suddenly driver *C*'s stalled car appears in the lane directly ahead of driver *B*. Driver *B* swerves into an "escape gap" in the next lane. Driver *A* takes a second or two to realize what is happening, can't find an escape gap, so he hits driver *C*'s stalled car.

The Blindgating Accident

You're following 6 car lengths back at 55 miles per hour . . .

. . . and car ahead veers to avoid stalled car. . . . You can't stop and cannot escape into crowded side lanes.

41

The Chain Collision

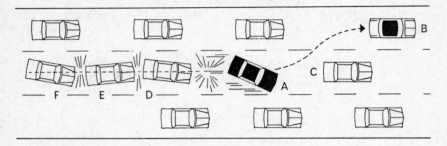

C stalls. B narrowly misses C. A applies brakes, skids to a stop, then gets hit by D, E, and F.

Another type of blindgating accident is even more serious.

It occurs when *A* sees *C* and applies his brakes in a panic stop and spins around. His car does not hit *C*. But *A* gets hit by several cars piling into his.

This produces chain collisions on fast new roads.

The only protection against blindgating accidents is vision. These revised car-length distances are designed to prevent your being blindgated:

On Town Streets and Slow Roads: Careful tests made for the Maryland Traffic Safety Commission and *Parade* show that one car length for each 10 miles of speed is still safe—but only at speeds up to 45 mph.

On Fast Highways: At speeds of 50 mph and over tests clearly show that the original one-car-length rule can become dangerous in dense traffic because in an emergency a driver may have no escape room on either side.

Here are some suggested new rules:

At 50 mph in very light traffic: On good, dry roads with few cars moving, at least a seven-car-length gap is desirable. In rain this gap should be increased.

At 50 mph in crowded traffic, dry road: Stay back at least nine car lengths if the road is dry. In rain leave still more space.

At 55 mph, medium traffic, dry road, all lanes in use: Here, because escape room is limited, a gap of 12–15 car lengths is needed and preferably even more.

At 55 mph in dense traffic: Road tests have shown that a great deal of room is needed to afford escape from possible emergencies. Following distance now should be not less than 18–20 car lengths.

The Right Gap

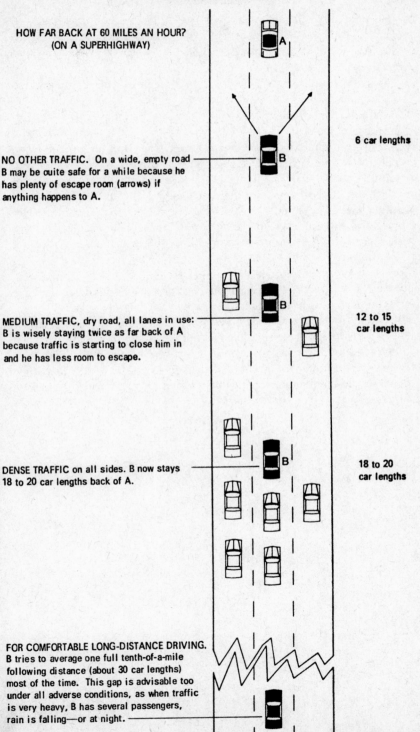

HOW FAR BACK AT 60 MILES AN HOUR?
(ON A SUPERHIGHWAY)

6 car lengths

NO OTHER TRAFFIC. On a wide, empty road
B may be quite safe for a while because he
has plenty of escape room (arrows) if
anything happens to A.

MEDIUM TRAFFIC, dry road, all lanes in use:
B is wisely staying twice as far back of A
because traffic is starting to close him in
and he has less room to escape.

12 to 15
car lengths

DENSE TRAFFIC on all sides. B now stays
18 to 20 car lengths back of A.

18 to 20
car lengths

FOR COMFORTABLE LONG-DISTANCE DRIVING.
B tries to average one full tenth-of-a-mile
following distance (about 30 car lengths)
most of the time. This gap is advisable too
under all adverse conditions, as when traffic
is very heavy, B has several passengers,
rain is falling—or at night.

At sustained, top legal expressway speeds: You are now entering speed levels at which *any* sudden stop or maneuver can be dangerous. On trips keep at least one-tenth of a mile—or more—between you and the car ahead whenever you can.

But won't many other cars "squeeze in" ahead of you if you stay so far back at speeds over 45 mph?

This is commonly believed by many drivers, but it just doesn't happen. In runs on busy roads when 60 mph was legal a test team found that surprisingly few cars squeeze in ahead, even when one car is following one-tenth of a mile behind another. The few drivers who did pull into the empty space usually pulled right out again and went on ahead. Rarely at the end of any ten-mile test run did the test car find itself more than eight car lengths back of its original position in line. Eight car lengths is only about two seconds' difference in time! Thus leaving a wide space ahead in super-road traffic was found to cause a driver virtually no delay at all.

The rush-hour commuter: an exception. The test team found that many excellent drivers in rush-hour city-expressway traffic seem to get along quite well with a six-car-length gap at expressway speeds.

But commuters are a special breed of high-pressure drivers. And for them the old one-car-length rule may not be quite so dangerous as it is for noncommuting drivers. Commuters who use the same fast road every day get to know its quirks and danger spots. Now and then they do miscalculate and bend a fender, but they rarely get trapped in serious mistakes.

CHAPTER VIII

MODERN DRIVING TECHNIQUES
FOR OLD-FASHIONED ROADS

DRIVING ON DIVIDED SUPERHIGHWAYS calls for one set of principles. Two-way roads require an entirely different set of principles. On two-way roads the smooth, even flow of traffic is missing. A driver must constantly expect the unexpected. Drivers must cooperate to keep each other out of trouble.

Here are a few major problems:

1. *Summer Foliage*. "Safe passing zones" on many two-way roads are marked off in early spring and before leaves begin to appear on trees. A maintenance engineer sighting down a narrow road at any given point may see that drivers have plenty of opportunity to see cars coming from the opposite direction. So his crew paint a broken line down the middle of the highway; passing is permitted.

But when trees come into full leaf, thick, leafy branches overhang the highway and cut off clear vision ahead. Passing becomes extremely dangerous. And yet the road is painted to invite passing. Before you pass on this type of road, make sure there really is enough room to get back in. Seasonal foliage hides countless driveways, side roads, curves, and playing children.

2. *Wrong-Side Driver*. The intoxicated driver who drives down the wrong side of the highway is a major hazard. Another dangerous wrong-sider is the driver who comes toward you on his own side of the road at high speed. He accidentally lets his wheels drop off the edge of the pavement. Frantic to pull back he oversteers. The car trips on the pavement edge, spins, then leaps across the pavement to your side—still coming very fast but now out of control.

What to do: It is important always to watch any car coming at high

The Hidden-Car Surprise

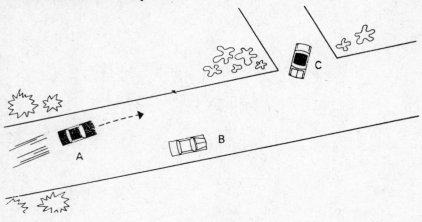

speed on a narrow road. Keep close watch, especially if the shoulders are in a condition to cause difficulty, i.e., if rough, muddy, or built several inches below pavement level. An expert soon learns to watch the general stability of any approaching car. He is alert to any car that (a) weaves slightly or (b) runs too close to the edge.

3. *Passing Surprises.* These come in many different categories. Here are some of the more common and what to do about them.

Hidden-Car Surprise. A pulls out of line at 50 mph and accelerates to 52, then to 55, in order to overtake B. But he has not noticed a small road or driveway on the left. C suddenly emerges from the left and A is hopelessly trapped. He cannot pull in ahead. There is no time to drop back.

What to do: The only way out of this is for B to cooperate and act fast. B must either accelerate very rapidly and permit A to drop back in line. Or B must brake very rapidly, slow down, and allow A to pull in ahead.

Right-Turn Surprise. A pulls out of line to pass, accelerates rapidly to 55 mph, and then begins to pull back in line ahead of B. But just then C slows down to 10 mph in order to make a right turn. A can't stop.

What to do: When C sees A pull out, he must cooperate. He should either abandon his plan to turn and accelerate rapidly—straight ahead— to relieve the "pressure" on A and B. Or if possible he can accelerate his right turn and leave the way open for A.

However, oncoming driver D can also do much to alleviate the situation. If *D* is an expert, he is automatically on the alert when he sees an approaching car (*C*) preparing for a turn—for *any* kind of turn! If *A,* *B,* and *C* are still some distance ahead, *D* can slow down sharply to give the situation time to resolve itself.

Left Turns. A driver who pauses in fast traffic to make a left turn stands an excellent chance of being hit.

What to do: One full mile before making a left turn from any two-way road start studying your mirror carefully. Know what cars are moving behind you. Are any coming especially fast?

The half-mile mark is the time to start estimating what the situation is going to be when you get ready to turn. This is also the time to look far ahead and start judging oncoming traffic too.

Will cars coming from the opposite direction be passing when you get ready to turn?

Is there a curve in the road anywhere near your turning point that may hide your car?

Are there hills near your turning point? Oncoming cars may be coming so fast they cannot stop. Hills change stopping distances considerably.

Is it raining? Is the road slippery?

What to do: If no cars are coming toward you from either direction, make the turn.

But *if* cars are coming fast behind you . . . and *if* one may be trying to overtake another . . . and *if* to make matters worse there are cars also coming from the opposite direction . . . *then* an expert driver simply abandons his attempt to turn. He continues on to a safe turn-

The Right-Turn Surprise

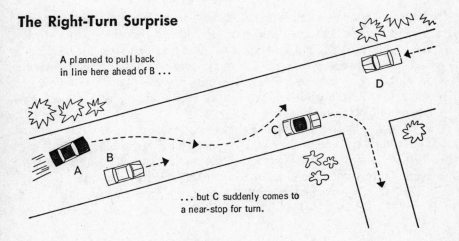

A planned to pull back in line here ahead of B . . .

D

. . . but C suddenly comes to a near-stop for turn.

around place, comes back, and then turns *right*. Or he pulls off the road at a safe place well in advance, waits for the fast traffic to clear, then makes his left turn. He never risks a left turn that blocks fast traffic.

Take an "Escape Reading." At 1:15 A.M. one morning the author was riding as observer in a Connecticut state-police car pursuing a drunken driver. The latter, racing north on the wrong side of a two-way highway, was heading toward certain head-on collision with some-one. We wanted to get ahead of him and stop him before he killed someone—or himself. To our dismay we saw headlights far ahead. Another car was coming directly toward the drunk. We didn't know until later that its driver was another trooper, trying to help us stop the drunken driver. The second trooper and the drunken driver were going to have a head-on collision. Shocked, we applied brakes and waited for the crash to happen.

It never did. In a remarkable display of fine driving, the trooper flung his car up a steep bank, swung around, and came down again—safe. Soon after that we caught the drunk.

The trooper escaped because he had formed a habit of studying the right side of any highway for emergency escapes. When the time came, he was able to see—in a split second and at night—a safe escape route.

You can learn the skill, too, by persistent practice. Train your eyes to "read" the roadside at a glance. On any road that you use regularly—learn to know the "escape spots" where you could steer with some hope of safety in an emergency.

DAY HEADLIGHTS ON COUNTRY AND SUBURBAN ROADS

Headlights can often be used to advantage even in broad daylight. You've noticed that most interstate bus drivers burn headlights all day long. They have found that vehicles with headlights on are noticed a fraction of a second sooner. This may seem like a slight difference but in months or years of driving it means a great margin of safety. In some Midwestern and Southern states thousands of auto drivers now use headlights even on sunny mornings.

Why this helps. Dr. Merrill J. Allen, in careful studies at Indiana University, concludes that many moving vehicles actually camouflage themselves against the highway background. White cars are fairly well seen, yet in winter even these become camouflaged against snow.

But headlights cause moving vehicles to stand out clearly. Further-

Day Headlights on Country and Suburban Roads

more, Dr. Allen found that passing drivers tend to give a lighted car a little more room.

In a year you may pass as many as 100,000 cars. A few inches of extra room on each pass adds up to an enormous increase in safety. Turn your headlights on and stand in front of your car; you will see something you may not have noticed. Most headlights look white at night. But in the daytime they look yellowish. This helps them stand out.

HOW'S YOUR PASSING?

You are driving 55 mph on a two-way country road and want to pass a car going 50 mph. How will you do it? Will your overtake make your passengers nervous? Will you bother the driver whose car you are about to pass? Or will you pass so smoothly that no one will realize that you've performed one of the most critical driving operations?

Passing: old style. Mainly to be avoided is the frantic passing *rush*. Some drivers dash out desperately, only to find themselves forced back

Passing Secrets

Be careful in a "high-crown" pass.

Bumps destroy passing control.

in line by oncoming cars. Then they dash out again and press the gas pedal hard while the passenger holds his breath in suspense. For such drivers every pass is a crisis.

When not to pass. Good passing is so easy with today's big engines that you can be more choosy about *where* you pass. You no longer have to take the first chance that comes along.

Most experts make it a rule *not* to attempt a pass in these three circumstances:

1. *When the road has a "high crown"* (when the road is much higher in the middle than at the edges). Passing on a sloping surface makes your car hard to control.

2. *When the surface is bumpy.* Bumps destroy the split-second timing needed in every pass. If bad, they can throw a car out of control.

3. *When there is less than a quarter-mile* of clear road in view. Even a short pass at road speeds may require a quarter-mile of clear road. And many passes in the 55 mph range require up to three-quarters of a mile.

The Troublesome "Pullout." An unsettling thing can happen if you employ the old-style "quick-pullout" pass. You pull up close behind a car, so that when the time comes, you can get around him quickly.

When you see a chance, you pull out suddenly. This can throw your car off balance just when you feed gas—and at a time when you need every ounce of stability you can get.

On a very narrow two-way road your car may actually run off the left shoulder.

Quick pullouts used to be necessary when engines were weak. But today they're to be avoided.

The "Drift-Out" Pass. To make this pass you *don't* pull up close behind the car ahead. You begin a drift-out pass farther back, let your car "drift" easily (rather than turn) toward the passing lane. At first, you don't move over entirely. You plant your left wheels near the center

How Far for a Pass?

Passing Technique

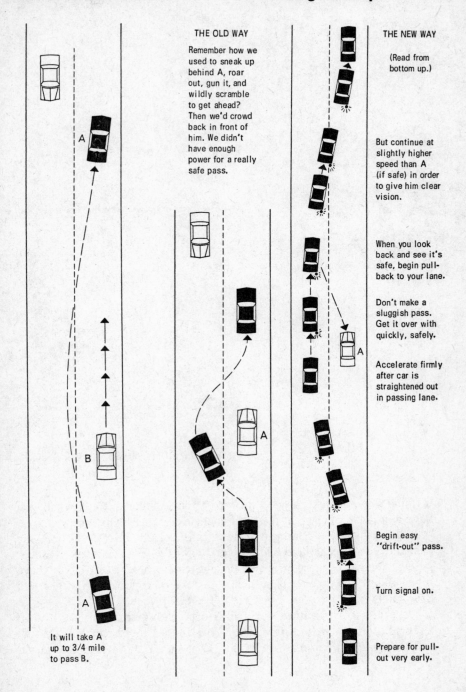

THE OLD WAY

Remember how we used to sneak up behind A, roar out, gun it, and wildly scramble to get ahead? Then we'd crowd back in front of him. We didn't have enough power for a really safe pass.

THE NEW WAY

(Read from bottom up.)

But continue at slightly higher speed than A (if safe) in order to give him clear vision.

When you look back and see it's safe, begin pull-back to your lane.

Don't make a sluggish pass. Get it over with quickly, safely.

Accelerate firmly after car is straightened out in passing lane.

Begin easy "drift-out" pass.

Turn signal on.

Prepare for pull-out very early.

It will take A up to 3/4 mile to pass B.

In rain the left (passing) lane on a superhighway is often more slippery.

Passing in Rain

Don't try to go through the "spray curtain."

dividing line and take a good look past the car ahead. Only when you have assured yourself that the road is clear do you begin to move up.

If the road ahead continues to look safe, you drift nearly all the way over into the passing lane and accelerate swiftly. Your car now is under perfect control because it is not turning or lurching. And if you have timed things right, there is still time to take your foot off the gas and drift safely back into the right lane—if necessary.

Once you're committed, get a pass over with fast. Don't slow down after you're back in the right lane. This annoys the driver you passed.

Don't smoke the other fellow out. Some cars pull back in line ahead of you and blast you with a noisy burst of exhaust smoke. This happens because drivers frantically trying to get back to safety kick down hard on the gas a second time. The result is what mechanics call "engine cleanout." A lot of smelly dirt is blown out and sucked in through your car's air intakes.

To avoid this, stay in the passing lane a bit longer, when safe to do so. And avoid tramping down hard on the gas when directly ahead of another car.

Passing in rain. The passing lane is often flooded with water because there is less traffic to "wipe" it dry. Do not attempt to pass at high speeds until you come to a stretch plainly blown free of excess water by other vehicles. (See "Drive the 'Tire Wipes,'" page 116.)

Use extra care when overtaking a fast truck in rain and look out for its curtain of spray (see page 117), which can block your view.

The "Come On" Signal. If a slow driver ahead on a narrow road waves to you to come on and pass in a blind spot, be on guard! Such well-meant hand signals have lured many drivers into trouble. If you decide to act on such a signal, be sure to allow yourself room to avoid an accident if the signal giver has failed to see danger coming.

Avoid the "fast-squeeze" pass. Some drivers rely too much on powerful engines and fail to allow enough distance for passing. Then when they see fast cars coming head-on, they attempt to "squeeze" back in line with a desperate burst of speed. A sudden last-second "speed burst" can actually make some cars respond sluggishly to steering. The driver may have difficulty returning to his side of the road in safety. Pass only when a pass clearly can be made without use of emergency power.

Speed-Burst Passing

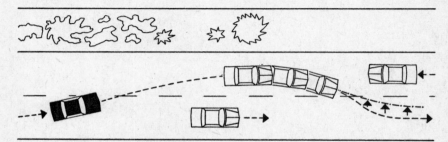

Sudden "speed burst" makes car want to stay in passing lane.
It is sluggish in turning back to proper lane.

PART TWO

FINESSE AND SOPHISTICATED
TECHNIQUES

CHAPTER IX

TALKING TO OTHER DRIVERS

MANY ACCIDENTS ARE CAUSED by lack of communication between drivers. One doesn't know what the other is up to—and the result is a mixup. Although automobiles don't have intercar communications yet, there is a way to "talk" to other drivers in a simple "language" of headlight flicks, horn sounds, hand signals, and even facial expressions.

Here's an introductory course in this automotive language. Learn it and add greater finesse to your driving.

On one trip the West Coast driving expert, Harold L. Smith, gave the author an interesting demonstration of "driver talk" and how useful it can be. In a five-state tour he "talked" often with other drivers at crossroads, in tight passing situations, even in the confusion of shopping-center parking lots. He talked with headlights, hand gestures, horn—even with the tilt of his head.

Eight "messages" he uses are:

1. *"I plan to turn left here!"* Thousands of cars get hit just before making left turns. The trouble is that the driver doesn't show clearly where he plans to turn. In one city the author interviewed a typical victim who had just wrecked his car and a woman's. This was his story: "We were on one of those four-lane, undivided suburban roads with traffic moving both ways. I was in the lane next to the center line, the woman was two hundred feet ahead of me. She flashed her left-turn signal. To me it meant, 'I will turn at the next corner.' Instead, she suddenly stopped in midblock before turning left into a bowling center. I hit her. The next car hit me."

To signal such a turn, start "drifting" your car gradually toward the center line after you switch on your turn light. Drift left an inch or two at a time. This drift will be noticed instantly by those behind you. It also "uncovers" your turn light to drivers several cars back. As the moment of turn approaches, tap your foot brake lightly to caution any driver who is still following too closely. In the last one hundred feet, when you are as close to the center line as you can safely come, your car's unusual position is saying clearly, "I am now ready to turn— *here!*"

2. *"I see you . . . and will help."* All of us on occasion find ourselves blocking the road for some faster driver who would like to pass. It would relieve tension if we could let him know, "I see you and will give you passing room as soon as a safe opportunity comes."

To convey this message, lift your head once or twice and glance in the rearview mirror. Even a slight tilt of the head is remarkably visible. It says, "I see you." At night it will also help if you reach up and adjust the mirror. The following driver sees this in the glow of his headlights. Now, as further courtesy, let your car drift to the right. This makes it easier for the other driver to watch for a safe passing zone and says, "I'll cooperate as soon as I can." Few drivers noting your courtesy will risk an angry, unwise pass.

There is a chance that the driver behind you will interpret your drift to mean, "If you want to pass, do it now." So, after the first drift, return your car to its normal position. The driver behind seems to understand. He drops back a safe distance and waits.

3. *"Danger in your lane! Prepare to stop."* Suppose that you pass a wreck which has occurred in an oncoming traffic lane. Seconds later, around a curve, you meet cars racing toward the wreck, unaware of danger. A pileup is imminent.

Such situations call for a signal that truck drivers use: rapidly flashing headlights. Truckers began blinking their headlights years ago to warn one another of speed patrols. Today the signal is an alert against any peril: wrecks, sudden ice, children in the road, washouts.

4. *"Danger in my lane! Don't hit me!"* Suppose you see, as drivers did one day in Connecticut, three boulders roll off a truck in front of 60-mph turnpike traffic. In such a crisis merely applying brakes is not enough to warn drivers behind you, who may simply rush around you toward disaster. To say, "Emergency!" pump the pedal in a series of fast, hard stabs to flash your brake lights. As soon as your car is under control, add a "flag-down" signal by waving your left arm in a wide vertical arc outside the window. Keep your brake lights flashing even after you've stopped.

We have tested this sequence of signals in several emergencies. In the case of the fallen boulders, we saw our flag-down wave copied instantly by drivers behind us. Within seconds, the message *"Danger!"* was relayed to cars far back.

5. *"I am watching out for you."* Horn blasts annoy and even anger

young bicyclists. Moreover, the cyclist may look over his shoulder in surprise or fright—and steer directly into your path.

The trouble is, most drivers sound their horns in warning when only four or five car lengths away. The best signal on a quiet street is a light, friendly "beep" sounded eight to ten car lengths (about half a block) away. If necessary, add a second beep, but space the two slightly, to keep a friendly, casual tone. Such early warnings give boys and girls time to adjust their steering calmly.

6. *"Please help me get in line."* All of us find ourselves blocked in side streets or driveways or parking lots by slow-moving traffic crossing our path. One reason no one wants to let us into the line is that too many of us demand to be let in. We point defiantly; we even jam our fenders into the line, then show the palm of our left hand to say, "Stay back there, mister!" We are, Smith says, sending the wrong message.

The trick he uses for getting into line: Choose one driver and look at him. And in that look—ask! Says Smith: "Try to get eye-to-eye contact. Give him a quick, friendly wave. And add a big, friendly smile—just in case." With such "talk," you rarely have to ask more than two drivers.

7. *"Thanks!"* When a driver makes way for you, thank him. It creates good feeling, makes for smoother driving. Many drivers use a half wave, half salute. Another signal, used by truck drivers, is two light taps on the horn, sounding almost like "Thank—you."

8. *"I'm sorry."* At a downtown traffic light in Delaware a daydreaming driver failed to start when the light turned green. Smith after a patient wait nudged his horn. The signal came out harsher than intended. The man glared back at us. Smith said, "Oh, oh, he's mad!"

At the next red traffic light we pulled up alongside that angry driver. Smith's hand came up in a cheerful little salute. As clearly as if he'd spoken, Smith was saying, "Sorry, friend, those things happen."

The other driver began to smile. And suddenly he was waggling back, a little salute which clearly said, "That's all right, forget it!"

Smith had extended the hand of friendship. And friendship is one of the greatest driving aids of all.

THE LANGUAGE OF LIGHTS

On an Eastern superhighway one rainy winter day a bridge toward which cars were hurrying at high speed suddenly iced up. One fast eastbound car started to spin and slide. Then two more cars slid. A bad pileup was imminent. Then a westbound driver saw the danger. Although it was broad daylight, he turned on his headlights and began flashing them at all eastbound cars that came toward him. Suddenly those drivers understood. He was using the truck drivers' "Trouble ahead!" signal. They slowed down. Soon all eastbound cars were proceeding cautiously across the bridge. That one westbound driver probably saved several cars from damage, maybe some lives.

The time to flash your lights is when you see a peril that fast drivers coming toward you might not discover in time.

Here are examples:

On a town street you pass a small child playing where she might be struck by cars.

On a narrow country road you pass children riding bicycles in the opposite lane. Then you round a blind curve and see several cars hurrying toward them at high speed.

In fog you pass an accident in the opposite lane and know that approaching drivers will not be able to see it in time to stop safely.

Like most emergency maneuvers, flashing your lights involves some risk. If done too slowly there is an interval of blindness. If done rapidly there is little loss of vision, for the lights are "off" for only a fraction of a second at a time.

The Courtesies. Certain manners are widely used by professional drivers. At dusk the sophisticated driver waits until no car is coming before turning on his lights. It is disconcerting to an oncoming driver to have lights suddenly flashed at him—even though his own lights are already on.

If you are driving uphill and see a glow at the top, you know that a car is coming up the other side. The experienced driver will usually lower his high beams before he sees the other car. And he can tell when the other driver responds, because the glow changes in intensity.

Some veteran drivers employ a signal that is appreciated by truck drivers. Let's say that a truck overtakes you on a wide modern road. After getting ahead of you he wants to get back in line, but he may be afraid of cutting you off.

Some drivers, after seeing him safely ahead, will flick their headlights once or twice, either up and down (night) or off and on (day). This tells him: "I am watching you and will help if you wish to pull in ahead of me."

The Driver Who "Won't Dim" His Headlights. People often ask, "Why do some drivers refuse to dim their lights? Why are they so rude?"

The answer is that the other driver usually isn't being rude at all. And he isn't "fighting" you with his lights. He is simply tired or confused. For many miles he has been lowering his lights for every car. But occasionally he forgets to return them to high beam. And so he is already on low beam as he approaches you. When you see him, you drop your beams to low. He kicks his dimmer switch to respond and kicks his lights up to high beam. You now think he has deliberately thrown glare directly into your eyes. But the fact is, he thought he was changing to low beams.

The Hilltop Illusion. Another misunderstanding may occur when driver *A* (see sketch) is approaching a hilltop, especially on a left curve. Driver *B,* coming from the opposite direction, crests the hill first. As *B* gets to the top, his lights are flashed full into *A*'s eyes, blinding him. Driver *A* naturally thinks that driver *B* has switched to high-beam head-lights. But the fact is, *B* has actually switched to low beams instead. So long as *B* was using high beams, his lights swept above *A* and caused no difficulty. But when he switches to low beams at the summit, the angle of the slope is such that his low beams hit *A*'s eyes.

Solution: Keep lights set on high beam for a few seconds longer as you reach a long hilltop, so that they will sweep the sky above an on-coming car until the last possible moment.

The tired (or drunk) driver is the main cause of glaring headlights at night. When a driver is exhausted, he sometimes forgets about light courtesies. It is dangerous to engage in a war of lights with him. Police have found that the fellow who won't dim is quite often not only tired but seriously intoxicated.

How to lick glare. If headlight glare bothers you, the cause may be a thin layer of dirt and film inside the windshield. This should be washed away.

An even worse cause is a sand-pitted windshield. A steady rain of sand or gravel blows off the top of many uncovered construction trucks. It can quickly opaque any glass.

Headlight Control

B switches to low beams at the wrong time.

High beams would go over A's car. Low beams hit A's eyes.

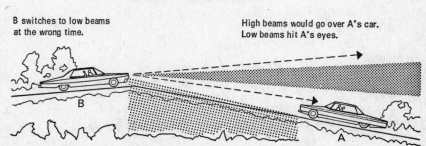

Windshield glare may also be caused by tailgating. All cars hurl back a fine, invisible rain of grit and dust. This cuts many small nicks in glass. Therefore, in order to keep a clear windshield that won't cause glare at night, avoid tailgating other cars or construction trucks.

If other drivers flash their lights at you when you are using low beams, your lows may be creating too much glare. This happens when cars are too heavily loaded in the rear. This causes low beams to be lifted and aimed toward other drivers' eyes. The cure: Shift some luggage from trunk to back seat. Or put bags on a roof rack in midcar position. (Even running with a half-full gas tank helps.)

THE LANGUAGE OF HORNS

There are three basic ways to sound a horn:

1. *The light knuckle tap* usually gives the most sensitive signal. It can be used on city streets when you quietly want to ask another driver to give you more passing room.

2. *The thumb punch* gives a slightly heavier, clumsier signal: "Move over and let me pass!" There's less courtesy in it.

3. *The whole-hand attack* is used to give a very forceful signal when needed—when you must signal another car to stop to avoid a collision.

When must you use (and NOT use) a horn? Some drivers don't know when they are required by law to use a horn—or when the law requires them not to.

"The law requires you to sound a horn whenever you overtake another vehicle." Is this really true? Certain states do require you to sound a warning when overtaking another vehicle. In other states a more practical law requires you to sound your horn only if there is evidence that some danger may develop. Know your state requirement.

What about big-city anti-horn laws? Most of them, it is generally agreed, were passed to prevent misuse of horns, which includes:

1. Sounding horn repeatedly when a traffic jam forms.

2. Sounding horn to hurry a driver who fails to start when a light turns green.

3. Using horn to "talk back" to a driver who has blown his horn at you.

4. Sounding horn as a means of summoning someone from a building.

5. Sounding horn unnecessarily in minor around-town traffic situations when it would be better to apply the brakes for a moment and slow down.

When you should use the horn. Here are situations in which use of the horn is clearly indicated:

1. When the driver ahead turns to his passenger and does not know you're passing.
2. When the driver ahead is obviously lost, in trouble, looking for an address, or trying to find a side road and fails to see you coming.
3. When you see several cars maneuvering in close quarters (as near a school, church, or factory) when you approach.
4. When you see bicyclists and realize that cars coming toward you are threatening them with a tight squeeze.
5. When you see someone stepping off the curb as you approach.

Horn warnings for children: right and wrong. To Harold L. Smith, the previously mentioned West Coast driving expert, give credit for the important discovery that a misused horn may create danger for bicycle riders. Children react with great surprise when a horn is sounded too loudly or at the last moment behind them. They glance over their shoulders. In so doing they inevitably pull their handlebars toward the left, and their bicycles turn directly in front of the approaching car.

Smith learned by experimentation to sound the horn lightly and early. When this is done, children usually pull safely to the right and almost never look back.

OTHER FACTS EVERY DRIVER SHOULD KNOW

Your Horn and the Truck Driver. Truck drivers sometimes cannot hear horns at all, especially at high speeds. Some truck cabs are so noisy that horns are simply drowned out. Never rely solely on your horn when overtaking a big truck. Catch the driver's eye in his mirror. Flash your lights if necessary.

The "Instant Thumb." In tight traffic it is always a good idea to keep an "instant thumb" on the horn sounder. This can save as much as a second of time—important if any emergency arises.

All Horns Are Different. No two respond alike. One of the first things to do when you sit behind the wheel of an unfamiliar car is: Find out how quickly the horn works. Some don't work at all unless pressed in a special way. Others are hard to find in a hurry.

CHAPTER X

"SPACE CUSHION" DRIVING

HOW EXPERTS AVOID TROUBLE

MOST EXPERT DRIVERS USE (some consciously, others instinctively) a system of "space cushion" driving that makes collisions all but impossible. This is why there are commercial drivers who log between 50,000 and 100,000 miles year after year, without trouble. The "space cushion" technique protects in fog, prevents sliding into collisions on icy roads, avoids those ridiculous chain pileups that often trap a dozen drivers at once.

The "space cushion" concept, developed by the author for a national magazine some years ago and now taught by many experts, is this:

You surround your car with a cushion of space in all directions, ample to absorb any emergencies that can occur ahead, on either side, or behind. Obviously there are moments when it is not possible to maintain such a cushion, as when other cars overtake you. But this is your target: to stay enclosed as much as possible in your own protective cushion of space. With due allowance for changing traffic conditions, you always return to it as quickly as possible.

A driver may say, "Well, it's easy enough to leave a space cushion in front of my car, but how can I stay away from cars that push up too close behind me?"

You will find part of the answer in "What to Do about Tailgaters" (page 93). Suppose the car behind you isn't leaving very much cushion between his car and yours?

On a narrow, busy road there is very little you can do about the fellow too close behind you. But you can at least be aware that the necessary space cushion behind you is missing for the time being. This awareness alone now offers you tremendous protection. You will tend to compensate by keeping a more alert lookout and you will find yourself constantly adjusting speed and position with other cars to minimize any emergency.

"Space Cushion" Driving

Car running habitually without space cushion will certainly be involved in a collision some day.

Car driving in space cushion has less chance of collision.

Thus the "space cushion" habit, once established, continues to work for you even when the cushion is imperfect. You will begin to make many little adjustments once the cushion is penetrated by cars ahead, on either side, **or** behind you. And you will make those adjustments in spite of yourself: You may sit more alert, keep a foot closer to the brake, search the road more carefully. You will certainly find yourself using brakes more conservatively. You may even develop new techniques of your own, such as moving your car left or right—as the situation requires—to help drivers behind you see better.

HOW TO HELP THE OTHER DRIVER SEE

Perhaps the greatest single cause of street and suburban-road smash-ups today is the inability of the driver behind you to see what's happening ahead of you. Take this case, for example:

A puts his brake on at the last moment and slows for a left turn. You (*B*) are caught by surprise, and get your brake on sharply. But

Better Visibility for the Driver behind You

WRONG: When you drive close to the center line, the driver behind you cannot see if someone stops ahead.

RIGHT: When someone ahead of you slows to turn or prepares to stop, pull slightly to the right so the driver behind you can see his brake light.

driver *C* sees only the sudden flash on your brake lights, can't stop, and hits you. You now hit car *A*.

To prevent this, when following another car in traffic it sometimes helps to adjust your car's position slightly to the right—so that the driver behind can see what's happening.

ALWAYS LEAVE YOURSELF AN OUT

This is one of the really great principles of good driving. The expert always has a place in view to which he can run when an emergency develops (as emergencies always do). He drives the way a helicopter pilot flies. A pilot always has one landing spot in view.

On a fast highway he spaces the distance to other cars in such a way that he can always swerve quickly right or left if an emergency develops. When other drivers hit cars ahead of them, he escapes safely to the shoulder or into a clear lane.

Coming down slippery hills he does not crowd up close to the cars ahead. He "lays back" so that if cars start to slide he can come to a soft landing on the shoulder and miss the others.

Moving up to red traffic lights on fast highways, he watches to see which way he can veer if someone comes up behind him too fast, out-of-control and unable to stop. He always tries to have an "out" waiting in any *tight* traffic situation.

KNOW THE "PATTERNS OF DANGER"

The way to avoid danger is to know the telltale signs and trouble spots long in advance. Here are situations that always alert the expert to trouble:

Any sudden puff of dust ahead on or near a high-speed road. Highway troopers say this is always a warning to slow down. It is one of the first accident-ahead signs that troopers watch for.

"Work area" signs or barriers on a high-speed road. Many of these are really terrible traps for unsuspecting drivers.

Most work areas are posted for 40-mph speed limits. But the slow rule is rarely enforced. And so drivers who would like to slow down, can't! They get "pushed" by fast traffic behind them. To protect your car, when you see the first signs or flags, determine early which lanes are closed. Move long before you have to into open lanes. Avoid the last-minute squeeze where wrecks occur.

Shopping-center entrances when located on fast, two-way streets cause the worst collision problems, police in some cities say. Entrances and exits often are side by side. Confusion results. Cars suddenly cutting across the street to enter the lots get blocked—in fast traffic—by cars coming out. And when this happens, they become sitting ducks.

The only suitable way to enter (or leave) a shopping-center lot on a fast street is by making a right turn. Beware of collision whenever you have to make a left turn across traffic either to enter or leave a lot.

The "Blind-Bridge" Trap. Many superhighway bridges are built with no escape shoulders. Traffic is wholly walled in—at super-highway speeds—between steel or concrete railings. To make matters worse,

The "Blind-Bridge" Trap

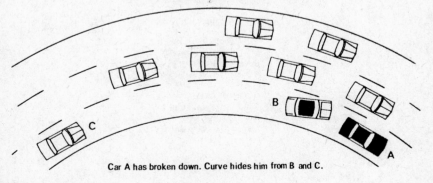

Car A has broken down. Curve hides him from B and C.

Leaving and Entering a Turnpike

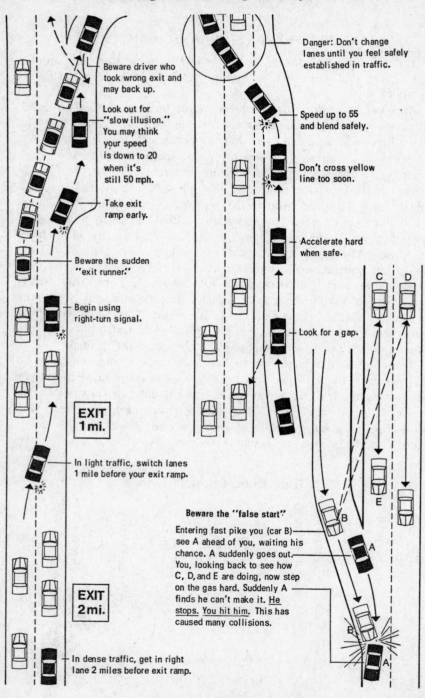

Beware driver who took wrong exit and may back up.

Look out for "slow illusion." You may think your speed is down to 20 when it's still 50 mph.

Take exit ramp early.

Beware the sudden "exit runner."

Begin using right-turn signal.

EXIT 1 mi.

In light traffic, switch lanes 1 mile before your exit ramp.

EXIT 2 mi.

In dense traffic, get in right lane 2 miles before exit ramp.

Danger: Don't change lanes until you feel safely established in traffic.

Speed up to 55 and blend safely.

Don't cross yellow line too soon.

Accelerate hard when safe.

Look for a gap.

Beware the "false start"

Entering fast pike you (car B) see A ahead of you, waiting his chance. A suddenly goes out. You, looking back to see how C, D, and E are doing, now step on the gas hard. Suddenly A finds he can't make it. <u>He stops. You hit him.</u> This has caused many collisions.

many bridges are built on curves. Drivers crossing such bridges, especially those in the No. 1 lane on right curves (or the No. 3 lane on left
curves), simply cannot see trouble ahead. It is good procedure never
to use the blind lane on a curving bridge without slowing down. Even
better—never use the blind lane at all. If you have to stop, someone
behind may not see *you!*

The Blocked-Exit Trap. Some superhighway exits cannot accommo-
date rush-hour traffic. A backup line of waiting cars results. Some are
forced to stop on the superhighway itself—and these sometimes get hit.

What to do: Try to determine in advance whether an exit ramp is full.
If it looks hopeless, avoid it. Continue to the next exit, then come back.

The Sudden-Stoplight Trap. Traffic lights don't exist on modern interstate routes, but they do block many older highways on which high
speeds are permitted.

But any traffic light on any fast highway is a potential collision trap.
Many stopped cars get hit from behind.

What to do: As soon as you spot a traffic light ahead, slow your car's
speed—long before you have to stop. Warn cars behind you by flashing
your brake lights repeatedly. Lay back until it appears that two or three
cars behind you have slowed. Now move slowly ahead, still leaving yourself a last-minute escape cushion. Try to time your driving so the light
will turn green and you won't have to stop at all.

The Accelerator Trap. One blunder causes unnecessary chain collisions at traffic lights. It is keeping a foot poised over the accelerator
pedal, ready for a quick start when the light turns green. If you now get
bumped from behind, your foot lifts, then slams down on the gas. This
hurls your car into the car ahead. To avoid this trap always guard your
rear when approaching or making a stop for a traffic light. Keep one
foot on the brake while stopped. Do not keep the right foot poised above
the gas when other cars are stopping behind you.

The Backing-Car Trap. When passing any exit on a superhighway,
always look for the vehicle that appears to be going your way but is
actually backing up because its driver missed the exit. On a fast road
any vehicle backing toward you in your lane always appears to be con-
tinuing straight ahead—until the last critical second. It's the most deadly
illusion of the highway.

The Misleading-Center-Line Trap. It is a good rule never to let a
"safe passing stripe" (a broken center line) lure you into passing when
you cannot see for yourself that the road ahead is clear. Many two-way
roads are painted to permit passing where it is dangerous to do so. Evi-

dently this is because maintenance crews have to mark the road in hours of light traffic when it looks safe. They don't seem to mark it according to what you cannot see when traffic is blocking the view.

If, when approaching a slight left-hand curve, you find the road marked for safe passing, always expect a car to pull out from behind another vehicle while approaching you. This is a moderate danger on 40–45-mph roads. But on faster roads it is a very serious problem indeed. The approaching driver, while thinking he is driving quite legally, could run you off the road—or hit you.

You may wonder: Why do the men who mark our roads make such mistakes? Part of the explanation lies in their attempt to give you as many safe passing zones as possible in order to keep you from being bottled up unnecessarily. Another reason is that many simply aren't trained engineers and don't fully realize the dangers.

CHAPTER XI

HOW TO STAY ALIVE ON THE SUPER ROADS

To RECORD THE SPECIAL SKILLS in freeway driving, the author drove seven hundred miles on the fast, superbly engineered New York State Thruway.

Then he drove for two days and a night with some of the world's best drivers, the troopers and engineers who patrol this very safe cross-country track.

His first discovery was that all troopers put extra air in their tires. A few extra pounds of air (don't overdo it) adds stability at speed; it also adds coolness, keeps tires safer.

He also learned: Old, out-of-condition cars can't stand hour after hour expressway speeds. They break down. And a "must" is good, fresh tires. Old dry ones come apart.

One of the professionals he rode with was Safety Officer Gene Sherwood, of the New York State Police. Sherwood sits tall at the wheel, handles his car decisively, and is the most alert driver the author has ever met. He drives the way a cat runs along a fence, calculating every inch. When Sherwood begins a pullout he does three things rapid-fire:

1. Checks his number one mirror (inside). Sizes up the entire road picture behind—and the rate at which cars are coming up, shuffling, switching lanes. Reason: He wants a "clear" behind him into which he can duck for safety if anything goes wrong ahead.

2. Checks number two mirror (outside left)—a quick, hard look. Who's back there in the blind spot?

3. You'd think that was enough. But Sherwood has learned. Now he turns clear around and looks backward over his left shoulder—for

Good Rules for Turnpike Driving

There's danger in wolf packs like this.

Old-fashioned: cars tailgating

Modern speed driving: more space

|← 12 car lengths to 1/10 mile →|

ONE MILE . . .

Be a loner.
Ride the
clear gap between
the packs.

Next wolf pack
often follows
about one
mile back.

Know the speed groupings
When the road is empty ahead and
behind, the 55-mph speed limit may
be okay, but . . .

55

. . . when you see traffic like this ahead
(and in your mirror), back off to 50 and
be ready for anything.

55

one fleeting second. Why? In that quick look he sweeps not only the blind spot but both lanes alongside to the left. He knows that cars now shuffle so fast at high speed that they can suddenly appear alongside you even after your mirror check.

A Faster Takeoff. When getting on a fast super road it is unsafe to drift lazily up the entrance ramp like a Sunday driver. You've got to treat the ramp as a pilot does a runway. It needs your full attention. To enter a fast pattern of traffic you need timing. Enter a super road only after making sure there's room in the pattern to blend without shoving somebody off his lane.

Some drivers don't work up enough speed, cut in too soon, and cause accidents. This isn't always their fault: some acceleration lanes are long and some are absurdly short.

So, when entering a fast super road, size up the length of the acceleration ramp first: On a fast road like the New York Thruway you must quickly get up to 55 mph for a safe blend.

Open Up a "Clear." Once in the main lanes, surround yourself today with a vast amount of space. Trans-Atlantic pilots have long insisted on lanes over one hundred miles wide. They know the importance of space. Yet we drivers run in bunches so close together that we could hold hands. Some troopers call this driving in "wolf packs."

But by any name, wolf-pack driving is for poor drivers only. The packs usually come by about once every minute—or about a mile apart. Stay in the gap between them. Open up a "clear" (1) ahead of you, (2) on either side and (3) behind you. At 50 mph and up you should always "be a loner" if you can.

KNOW THE ALERTS

When a trooper on a super road sees a puff of dust ahead he gets ready for a sudden stop. Dust, as previously noted, is often a sign someone has just had an accident—or is about to.

Another alert that troopers recognize is a sudden cluster of cars where there was a clear road far ahead. Another: small scraps of wood, metal or tire. Slow down.

Use an early-warning signal if you do sense possible trouble ahead. Tapping your brake a few times tells drivers behind you: "I'm not stopping yet, but I see something ahead. Stay alert."

Back off (slow down) early when you know there's trouble. Never risk getting involved in a fast stop among many cars traveling at high speed. To avoid it, start flashing brake lights to get cars behind you under control before they plow into you. And add a big flag-down arm-wave. Drivers pay more notice to waving arms than to lights.

And while slowing down, keep a constant mirror-check and leave space for the other fellows trying to stop behind you.

Don't pass (or be passed) under bridges if you can help it. On any pike where ice forms, troopers told me, you should try never to come abreast of another car as you go into an underpass. That's where ice patches send many cars spinning. Half a mile before an underpass, check mirrors and if you see someone about to overtake you, speed up or slow down so you won't have him alongside in the slippery spots.

Never change lanes to pass on a high-speed curve, especially a right curve. Reason: as you pull out, "centrifugal force" tries to toss you off the road.

Get passes over with—fast. At high speed, a sluggish pass can take a full mile. That means you're exposed to collision for a mile. Once you start a pass, accelerate safely and legally, but get on with it.

Watch for "marginal friction," especially in the right lane, when passing through towns. Cars entering from the right create eddies in traffic. Troopers have a rule: "Guard your right when passing entrance ramps." To keep things safe for all, help make room for any driver you see trying to enter from a ramp.

If a tire goes flat on a bridge, or where there's no shoulder, keep right on going to a safe escape area. Ruin the tire rather than risk collision by stopping in a lane.

In a high-speed blowout troopers have two tricks: (1) They train themselves to expect the explosive "pow!" that comes with some blow-outs and also the dull "bloop-a-bloop" heard with others. (2) They never let the car veer even for a split second. They keep the wheel centered, lock elbows and fight to keep arrow-straight control.

Operational Plan for an Exit. When you feel yourself getting hungry, troopers say, it is wise to plan your exit maneuver at least five miles in advance. If traffic is light, look for the sign that says "Exit [or Service Area] 1 Mile." As you pass that sign swing into the right lane, then pick up your exit ramp.

But when traffic is heavy, watch for the earlier sign that, on many pikes, says: "Exit 2 Miles." To avoid a last-minute scramble, this is your signal to switch.

Above all, guard against the dangerous "exit runner," the fellow who stays in the fast lane until the last minute, then cuts across traffic in front of you and squeezes down the exit ramp. He's caused lots of accidents.

CHAPTER XII

"COMPUTER DRIVING" AND HOW TO READ THE ROAD AHEAD

COMPUTER DRIVING

DRIVING A FAST HIGHWAY is like landing a jet airliner on a runway. There are split-second decisions. Problems rush toward you at a furious rate. You may make as many as fifty or more small steering adjustments in a single mile. In a five hundred-mile trip that's 25,000 small decisions that involve steering. Other thousands involve acceleration, braking, passing, and so on.

To psychologists, driving has actually become a computer operation— although few drivers realize it.

U.S. Department of Transportation experts say a good driver actually computes his way through all these decisions for mile after mile. In a single mile a really good driver's eyes see and note the progress of as many as a thousand objects as they flow toward him. All these data go to a personalized built-in "computer" in his brain. The computer does an astonishing job of calculating what needs to be done. Then it sends a steady "readout" of instructions to his hands and feet.

Much of this happens without the driver's awareness. While he is concentrating on other aspects of driving, his helpful computer may automatically tell his hands to turn left exactly 24.7 degrees for a curve. It may also direct his foot to apply 2.06 pounds of pressure to the brake for exactly four seconds.

HOW TO MAKE THE EYES SEE MORE

But the poor driver fails to "compute" his way along because his eyes don't gather enough information. Often he steers by fixing his eyes on a point in the road about 150 feet ahead. He sees little else.

Visual Alertness

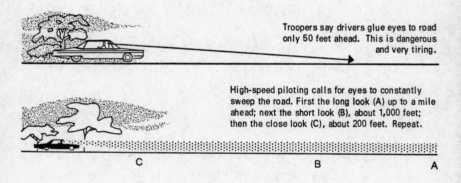

Troopers say drivers glue eyes to road only 50 feet ahead. This is dangerous and very tiring.

High-speed piloting calls for eyes to constantly sweep the road. First the long look (A) up to a mile ahead; next the short look (B), about 1,000 feet; then the close look (C), about 200 feet. Repeat.

Or at night he may focus his eyes on the taillight of the car he is following. He relies on it to lead the way. How can this kind of driver learn to see more? The answer lies in . . .

The Eye-Sweep Technique. While the poor driver fixes his eyes steadily on that point ahead, the expert's eyes rove constantly, sweeping back and forth as well as looking ahead and behind.

The Long Look, the Near Look and the Close Look. No driver's eyes, especially at highway speed, should ever watch one spot for more than a second or two. They should skip constantly. And every few seconds they should make a "long look" (to a distant point ahead), then an "intermediate look," and then a "close look" to the pavement just ahead of the car.

In addition, the eyes need to swing rapidly and repeatedly from side to side.

The Cone of Vision. In effect, then, the expert's eyes are constantly sweeping across every detail in a cone-shaped slice of landscape. They must know everything that is happening in that cone that can possibly affect him. If for a moment this becomes impossible (as when curves, bridges or large trucks block the view), then a slowdown is called for or at least a special alertness until full vision is restored.

The Cone of Vision

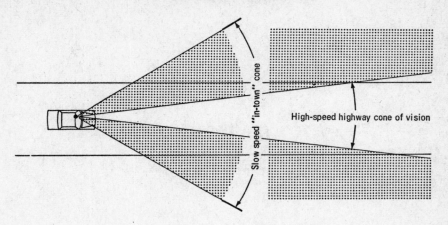

Slow speed "in-town" cone

High-speed highway cone of vision

Your Eyes over the Road

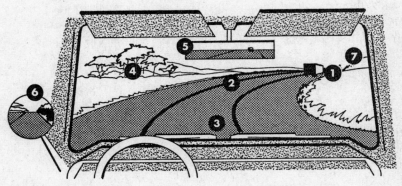

1. Take a reading on events to come, 30-60 seconds ahead.

2. Check road for obstacles.

3. Check road close ahead. This gives you sense of speed, control, position.

4. Read the left side of the road.

5. Check rear mirror.

6. Check outside mirror at intervals for security.

7. Return eyes to the long look one-half mile to a mile ahead.

CHAPTER XIII

HOW TO "READ" THE OTHER CAR—

AND ITS DRIVER

THE EXPERT MAKES it a point to spot the "unpredictables" in traffic. Then he gives them wider space in passing. He never plans any maneuver that will depend for its success on another driver who may maneuver without signaling (or may not act in accord with his own signals).

The expert also keeps a sharp eye on other cars so that he can tell whether they are under full control. He learns to judge by their movements whether they may weave out of line at some critical moment. He notes small details such as smoke from the exhaust pipe. A burst of gray smoke or a long trail of thick blue smoke means that a car is accelerating sharply (and an accelerating car is often not under full control). Lazy puffs of bluish smoke mean a car is slowing down. And a decelerating car, likewise, is always an unpredictable one.

The expert even notes how another driver sits at the wheel. Is he alert and attentive? This tells a good deal. Is his car sloppy-looking? A dirty, battered car often has poor brakes, thin tires, and a slow-to-respond steering system. It often has a driver who is careless about his driving habits too! In general a crisp, clean car, well-balanced and moving smoothly, will rarely present a problem to you. You can tell by decisive handling when a driver knows exactly what he wants to do.

WHAT TO WATCH FOR IN THE CAR AHEAD OF YOU

Beware the dawdler or the uncertain driver. This one is looking for a friend's house in an unfamiliar part of town. Now he thinks he's found the street. He signals for a right turn, even turns his head and looks toward the right. But just then his wife says: "No, they told us to turn

The Indecisive Driver

The Drifting Driver

left. Remember?" She points left. Caught off guard, he panics a little and away he goes into a quick left turn with right blinker still flashing merrily! Never trust an indecisive driver.

Always watch the left front wheel of a car coming toward you on a narrow two-way road. It can give you fast warning of a sudden turn because front wheels turn a fraction of a second before a car itself.

Note any instability in the car ahead of you. All cars drift slightly— and normally—from side to side in their lanes. You can note this in the tracks they leave on a rainy pavement. However, most drivers tighten up their steering and maintain an arrow-straight course just before meeting and passing another car.

If the driver ahead of you fails to do this, be cautious about overtaking.

Learn about the driver ahead of you by the way he sits. We have already observed that an alert, erect driver is usually cause for confidence. But a driver who sits very low and peers through the wheel is not. And a driver who leans his weight noticeably against the left door and has one hand on the car top is apt to make sudden turns, sudden accelerations, sudden stops. Sometimes he has time to signal and sometimes he doesn't.

A driver whose lady friend is sitting in midseat next to him (or has her arm around his shoulders) may be unpredictable in a crisis.

Check the appearance of a truck's tires before you overtake it, if you can. A truck tire that blows out while you are passing it is a frightening thing. If a tire looks frayed, avoid passing or else give extra room and get your pass over quickly. Don't follow close behind a truck if one tire is flapping or disintegrating. Huge retreads breaking off can cause trouble for cars.

WHAT TO WATCH FOR IN THE CAR BEHIND YOU

Once if drivers saw danger ahead, they stopped with no thought to what might be happening behind. The general philosophy was: It was up to the fellow behind you to look out for himself. If he hit your rear bumper, the law usually said he was to blame, and that was that. There was a further factor: Cars were designed with small rear windows. You couldn't see out the back very well, anyhow!

But all that has changed in the era of high speed. If you stop on the pavement (or even if you slow down sharply), you're in danger of getting hit. Thus, in the expert driver's mind danger ahead instantly spells danger behind.

When danger threatens, the inexperienced driver immediately puts on his brakes and checks his mirror to see what cars back there are doing and whether they can stop in time. And while he is doing this his car may get caught in a giant nutcracker—between an accident ahead and a pileup of skidding cars behind.

But when the expert sees danger ahead, he already knows exactly what's happening behind him. That's because his eyes have been relentlessly watching the road back there. He drives the road behind him

Danger Ahead Spells Danger Behind

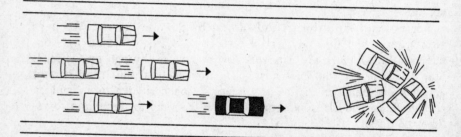

Moving Cone of Safety

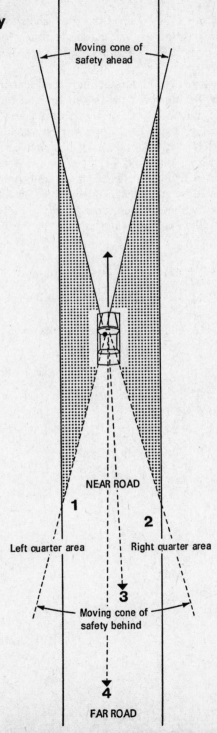

Moving cone of safety ahead

NEAR ROAD

1

2

Left quarter area

Right quarter area

3

Moving cone of safety behind

4

FAR ROAD

almost as much as he does the road ahead. When danger strikes, he is already in position to take evasive action. He knows that a crisis ahead means a crisis behind—and it's often too late to check the road back there.

To keep posted on cars behind, some experts take a "rate-of-change" reading in the mirror at least four times a minute. And in dense traffic their eyes may do a mirror-check once every ten seconds.

In specific terms, the expert's eyes watch four main "checkpoints": (1) his left quarter area, (2) his right quarter, (3) the near road directly behind him, and (4) on a highway, the far road from one-tenth of a mile to a full mile back, depending on conditions and speed. (In a city the far-road checkpoint might be a block behind.)

And so, while maintaining a cone of safety ahead, he is at all times checking a similar but wider cone of safety behind.

CHAPTER XIV

UNSEEN HIGHWAY FORCES THAT AFFECT
YOUR DRIVING

Engineers at Purdue University have found that a good many odd forces work on your car—and even on you—when you drive. Some are pressures that Professor Joseph Oppenlander compares to high electric voltage. Others are like forces that buffet jet planes: shock waves, turbulence, G-forces, and friction.

When these forces take over, you no longer are the real driver of your car. You become only a helper trying to keep control.

A good example is the driver who finds himself skidding into a tangle of cars. He brakes hard but can turn neither right nor left because of vehicles on both sides. He is at the mercy of several different pressures and all he can hope to do is guide his car a little.

1. *Shock Waves.* They get started whenever fast traffic comes to an abrupt stop and they move back down the road against oncoming traffic.

Example: Suppose that you are driving west at 55 mph on U.S. highway 66. Two miles ahead two cars bang together and block the road. Suddenly everything at that spot comes to a full stop.

But now something else happens that few drivers are aware of. You continue westward at 55, blissfully unaware that a dangerous wave of stopping cars is rushing to meet you. In dense traffic it may come at 40 mph or better. And so you are closing with it at 95 mph, the combined speed of the wave and your car.

The front of this wave is an almost solid wall of suddenly stopped cars. Your first alert is a flash of brake lights. And then, without warning, cars all around you have their brakes on and are skidding. A huge crash may result—and yet it is really only an echo of the pileup that

83

happened minutes before and two or three miles ahead. You've met the shock wave!

Purdue's engineers don't try to tell you how to avoid such a wave; they're content to warn that it exists. To keep from getting trapped by one, you must constantly scan far ahead in heavy traffic—as far as you can see.

And you must keep in mind a continuous "flow picture" of all that's happening, even a half-mile ahead. Watch for the first sign of a wave—bunching of cars or flashing brake lights.

Not all shock waves come to meet you so fast. After a minor accident, a wave of stopping cars forms and may continue to block cars near the same spot even after damaged cars are towed away. State troopers report seeing cars still stopping or slowing because of such a wave for thirty minutes or more after the road has been reopened. This wave moves very slowly upstream toward you.

2. *Turbulence* is a disorderly force that can really push you around. It breaks out, according to Professor Harold L. Michael, of Purdue University, whenever any obstacle disturbs the smooth flow of traffic. It's first cousin to the turbulence that tosses airliners when anything upsets the smoothness of the air.

Example: Suppose driver M ahead of you suddenly runs out of gas on one of those superhighway bridges which have no shoulders. Having no refuge zone, driver M coasts a few yards, then stops right in traffic.

What results is the same thing that happens when air (or water) molecules try to pass an obstruction in a pipe. Each car becomes a "molecule" fighting for room. Each, trying to squeeze past the stalled car, jostles others. It may not hit the others but it forces them aside. Accidents result.

Turbulence deprives you of freedom to decide where to go. You are at the mercy of the raw traffic forces. And sometimes you're helpless to resist.

The expert knows where to look for turbulence. He shifts lanes long before he has to—in order to escape it. Drivers who *don't* anticipate turbulence sail right into the thick of it and find themselves in its clutches.

Where to look for it. Severe turbulence is generated at highway entrances and exits, intersections and driveway entrances; around stalled or slow-moving vehicles; and by left-turning cars that are forced to stop in the fast lane.

Turbulence

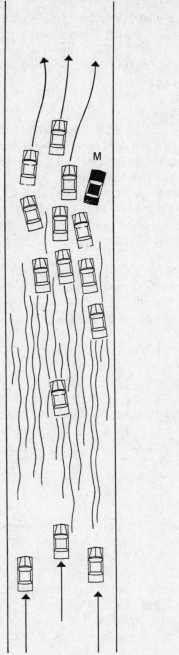

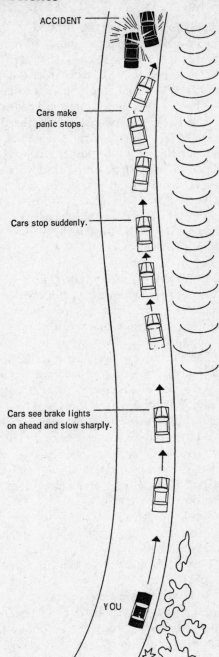

ACCIDENT

Cars make panic stops.

Cars stop suddenly.

Cars see brake lights on ahead and slow sharply.

M

YOU

3. *G-forces* throw you around at the wheel, interfere with steering and braking, and can seriously affect your driving. Here's when they occur:

Whenever you brake too hard. (G-force can throw your whole weight on the brake—and stop you faster than you want to.)

Whenever you accelerate too suddenly.

When you turn too fast as on a sharp superhighway exit.

On a fairly sharp turn, Dr. James Schuster, of Purdue University, discovered, your car is pushed sideways by a G-force equal to more than one-tenth its weight. On a tight turn centrifugal force can cause you to slide on the front seat unless you have your seat belt buckled.

Note: Strictly speaking, G-force is the force exerted by the acceleration of gravity, or roughly thirty-two feet per second per second. This is known as one G. But any force that tends sharply to accelerate, stop, or turn an object (such as the human body) has come to be loosely called a "G-force."

4. *"Friction" forces* also affect your driving. Anything near the road's edge, engineers say, "throws an invisible punch at you." Sometimes the punch is purely psychological; sometimes it is physical and your car is actually blocked. But whatever it is, like friction that works in any machine, it slows you down.

The Purdue engineers have found that the mere presence of a roadside store slows you one-half mile per hour.

Example: While driving 50 mph suppose you enter a one-mile stretch in which there are five stores and five gas stations. The presence of ten establishments will tend to force your speed down to 45 mph. Almost any object near the road causes "friction," even poles, signs, parked cars, overhead bridges, side-road (or driveway) entrances, and pedestrians. A big billboard slows you one-quarter mph.

Besides these, it is now known that several other "resistance forces" also slow you. Among them:

Sun in your eyes.

A passenger in your car (because you talk, and talking drivers usually travel more slowly).

Curves. A mild curve can drop your speed (without your realizing it) by 3 mph.

Roadside interference is known to engineers as "marginal friction." And like mechanical friction it actually makes heat! This shows up in your tires and brakes. And according to Professor Milton E. Harr, "It may even show up in you. . . . You actually get 'hot under the collar' in trying to maneuver through an area of severe friction."

Friction

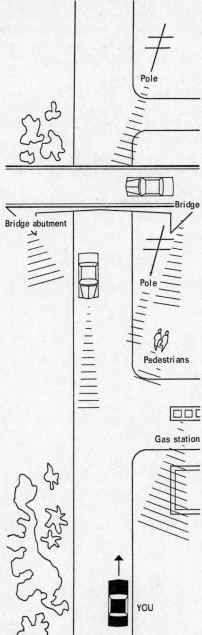

How psychological "friction" forces tend to push at you and slow you down.

Pressures That Speed You Up. While measuring forces that slow you down, engineers discovered that other forces are also at work today to speed you up. Some may make you go faster than you want to go:

Out-of-state drivers. Since they don't stop so often as local cars, they tend to "push" traffic faster.

Big trucks. They too tend to go faster and to push traffic.

Downgrades. For every 1 percent of downgrade you go one-tenth of a mile per hour faster.

Good roads, easy curves, and a wide, spreading view ahead also speed you up.

One problem still baffles the engineers, who now want to find out more about it. It's the traffic jam. "It breaks all our rules," says Purdue's Professor Harr. "None of our formulas work. We now call it a traffic 'nervous breakdown!' "

CHAPTER XV

HOW TO FIGHT FATIGUE

DRIVERS FOR YEARS have been told: When tired and sleepy, open windows, turn on the radio, stretch, shout, sing, drink coffee, stop for a meal. These ideas may work—temporarily. But they never work for very long, and they can lure you into serious trouble.

Such anti-sleep "tricks" can actually increase your danger, according to Dr. Alfred Moseley, a Boston traffic psychologist. After four or five minutes of apparent relief, sleep moves in again, and this time it suddenly overwhelms you—with no warning, no nodding head, no sudden pre-sleep quiver.

The good driver when sleepy will stop and let sleep take over, Dr. Moseley says. Plan in advance for one or two "sleep breaks" on any long trip.

If sudden need for sleep assails you when driving, there's only one safe thing to do—sleep! Stop in a safe place, such as a service-area parking lot or an all-night gas station. Lock your car. Turn the motor off. Lower one or two windows slightly for air. Sleep.

A sleeping bag or light mattress in a station wagon affords wonderful rest. Some cars are equipped with front seats that tip back flat and can be converted into a bed for naps. Or you can stretch out on the back seat of almost any car and nap with feet elevated and resting comfortably on baggage. This stretched-out position, many drivers find, gives more rest than sleep sitting up.

After a nap of fifteen to forty-five minutes you will awaken refreshed. However, it is possible that after driving a half hour or so, sleep may once more assail you. In that case, stop and take a second nap. After that you should be able to drive for hours. Two naps sometimes seem as restorative as a night's sleep.

On any long trip, as when taking a vacation, it is wise to take along a pillow or two and a blanket. These add enormously to comfort and the ability to get real rest in a brief sleep break.

It is true that a meal sometimes helps eliminate fatigue. But that may be because a driver is hungry rather than sleepy. If a driver has been running short on sleep, a meal may make him feel better temporarily. But later he may be even sleepier. After his meal he should take a nap.

Besides the risk of getting hurt or hurting someone else, there is a dollars-and-cents reason for not driving when you feel your eyes wanting to close. Some courts have held that a driver who allows himself to go to sleep at the wheel is guilty of negligence; and negligent drivers have sometimes had a good deal of trouble getting insurance companies —or anyone else—to help pay their damage bills.

How Air Conditioning Helps Good Driving. Air conditioning also helps to fight fatigue and reduce accidents. Many drivers use it to relieve the sun heat that pours in through sloping windshields and windows.

A driver who is uncomfortable on a hot, muggy day tends to make mistakes. He may become irritable and, on a long trip, tired. If because of heat he must keep windows open, the constant buffeting of wind is annoying.

By contrast, a driver in a cool, comfortable car will be less fatigued, less irritable, and less apt to make mistakes.

CHAPTER XVI

LEFT-FOOT BRAKING

B<small>RAKING WITH THE LEFT FOOT</small> instead of the right is a controversial subject. Some experts consider it dangerous. But others, who use it regularly, find it has definite advantages.

What left-foot braking is. In a standard-shift automobile, your right foot controls both accelerator and brake. Your left foot works the clutch.

In a clutchless automatic-transmission car, the left foot is free for use on the brake if desired.

DISADVANTAGES OF LEFT-FOOT BRAKING

Even learning it has some dangers. Until the left foot becomes "sensitized," beginners accidentally jab the brake too hard, lock wheels, and cause sudden stops. This error may be made several times during the first few days of learning.

Using left-foot braking has some dangers. During the first few months the error of jabbing the brake pedal too hard can recur now and then. In addition there is always a chance that in a moment of emergency you might not be able to decide *which* foot to use.

Confusion can occur at night. The left foot cannot handle both the dimmer switch and the brake at once. Right-foot braking is often necessary at night.

Wear on the brakes. One objection raised to left-foot braking is that it encourages a driver to use his brakes more and that it costs more to keep them in repair.

It's habit-forming. If you learn left-foot braking and then switch to a standard-shift car, you may have to unlearn it.

ADVANTAGES OF LEFT-FOOT BRAKING

Faster braking in emergency. With the left foot always ready over the brake pedal you can apply brakes much sooner. This is especially useful when driving through crowded streets. If a child darts out behind a parked car, the left foot can actually apply the brakes before the right foot can be lifted off the gas. The time and distance saved might easily save a child's life.

When "dragging the brakes" can help. Some drivers intentionally let their left foot rest lightly on the brake pedal when passing through crowded streets (see page 23). Thus, even though the right foot is feeding a little gas, the left foot already has the car under taut control, ready to slam down hard in a fraction of a second for any emergency, such as a running child.

This practice also makes split-second braking possible in any tight highway situation, as when squeezing past a construction area.

Which method should you learn first (if you are a beginner)?

Answer: Learn the right-foot method. Left-foot braking is an improvement that can come later. Most state motor-vehicle departments still require driving-license applicants to use right-foot braking.

A good driver will eventually learn to use either foot on the brake, depending on conditions.

Left-Foot Braking

CHAPTER XVII

GETTING ALONG WITH OTHER DRIVERS

"THE OTHER DRIVER" can be a problem at times. But it should be remembered (as stated earlier) that his faults are often exaggerated. As a rule he is exactly like you. He has the same problems, makes the same blunders, has the same good intentions—and gets misunderstood.

When he bothers you, the offense is usually not intended. A few are troublemakers. But the intentional troublemaker is rare indeed.

WHAT TO DO ABOUT TAILGATERS

Every driver now and then finds himself plagued by cars and trucks that pull up close behind and all but touch his bumper. There are four types of tailgater:

1. *The natural follower* is easiest to avoid. This driver just likes to follow anyone who will lead the way. He lets you do the work of driving for him. You see all the problems. You decide when to slow down. This devoted follower is often daydreaming, and may even be trailing you hypnotically. He's a very real menace because if you suddenly have to stop, he may hit you. To get rid of him some experts try slowing down. However, he may be so unaware of what's happening that he will merely slow down too!

What to do: Stop in a safe place, let him go by and fasten his attention to some other car. After this, regain your speed and, if safe and proper, pass him. In his unthinking way he usually stays loyally behind his new friend!

2. *The sociable driver.* This one simply likes company on the road. He may fall in behind you on an empty superhighway and stay with

you for miles, and miles, blocking your view in your rearview mirror. (Often he's a tourist.) Unlike the "natural follower" this driver isn't letting you do the work. He'd just rather travel with someone else.

What to do: If his close presence bothers you, try varying speed. Or on an empty superhighway you might try switching lanes when safe. This often seems to break the friendly but dangerous attachment, and the other driver will usually drop back. Or when you pull back into your lane, he may put on speed at last and pass you.

3. *The "reasonable pusher."* This is the fellow on a narrow road who is a tailgater only because you go too slow and *make* him a tailgater. He's caught behind your car, and there are no passing zones. If the speed limit is 50, he wants to go at least 48, yet here we are cruising along, talking, and letting our speed wander between 38 and 44.

What to do: This tailgater is trying to "push" us by staying so close. But he's easily satisfied. All you have to do is speed up a little—say, to a steady 48. Usually he won't even try to force you up to the speed limit. If you don't want to speed up (or for some reason can't), it's easy to cruise to a safe shoulder, let him get ahead, then pull back on the road. You've lost only a few seconds.

Always let a tailgater get ahead when you can. He may have a good reason for being in a hurry.

In a Western state a driver on a narrow road refused to make room for a car behind him. There were no safe places for passing and he delayed the other car for miles. Finally the car overtook him, and only then did he see that its license bore the letters "MD."

Twenty minutes later the driver reached home and saw the MD plates again. The driver he'd delayed had been a physician on a call to attend his own baby daughter.

4. *The unreasonable pusher, or "bulldozer."* Get rid of this follower by all means. He is the driver who rushes up to your rear bumper, clearly trying to scare you out of his way even though you are maintaining full traffic speed and have cars ahead of you.

He is a threat for several reasons: He is sometimes a quarrelsome driver who feels entitled to "demand" the road. And he is sometimes intoxicated or under the influence of drugs or "pep pills."

In a car he is menace enough; but if driving a truck or bus, he is even more dangerous because he can't stop so fast as you can. In case of a panic situation at 55 mph a good driver can usually stop a car in three hundred sixty feet or less. But it often takes five hundred feet to stop a big truck.

What to do:

1. Pocket your pride and switch to another lane as soon as possible (if safe).

2. Speed up if possible (and legal), but only if he does not continue to pressure you at the higher speed.

3. But suppose you can't change lanes? It is sometimes impossible to switch from a fast to a slow lane because of danger to other cars. If so, try slowing cautiously—to give the "bulldozer" a chance to pull around you and go ahead.

4. If nothing else works, try using your lights. In daytime put head-lights on. He will see your taillights, will know what you've done, and may slow down—because no bulldozer wants to see you do anything that will attract the attention of passing police. In extreme danger it may pay, too, to turn on your four-way "hazard flashers." (Running with flashing lights is forbidden in some states and this should be noted.) Flashing red taillights have a powerful cautioning effect on all drivers, and he may leave you alone.

WHAT TO DO ABOUT THE SLOW DRIVER
AHEAD OF YOU

Everyone dislikes the "slow driver" who plugs the road and delays lines of traffic. But before you join the "hate the slow driver" club, you'll be interested in what investigators found out about him.

In North Carolina the State Highway Patrol and the author decided to learn the truth about slow drivers. Why do some drivers block every-body? Do they do it for meanness? Are they careless or selfish?

Whenever a slow driver was seen holding back a line and creating danger, he was stopped and was asked frankly: "Why were you going so slowly? Didn't you see all those other drivers back there waiting to get around you?"

For three days the patrol stopped drivers and the author interviewed them. The results were surprising. No one got a ticket for slow driving. In every case the driver had good reason to be going slowly. Most were people who were old or sick or crippled or under heavy medication. Some were in old cars that couldn't (and shouldn't) have gone much faster. Some seemed mentally dull. Several were drunk (and these were arrested for driving while under the influence of liquor).

But in three days not a single "mean driver" was found who was deliberately making everyone else go slow.

Such drivers do exist, but there aren't many.

If YOU ever must become a slow driver, here is what you should remember. The slow driver is a danger as well as a nuisance because he creates "knots" of cars, and this forms accident situations.

Other drivers are usually willing to follow him for a mile or two, but eventually they lose patience and try to get ahead. Accidents start happening when drivers—including some who may be hurrying to appointments, hospitals, or airports—pull out of line and make desperate attempts to work forward. Such drivers often meet cars coming from the opposite direction. Or they cut in and sideswipe cars in the slow line.

Although accidents happen behind him, the slow driver himself may never have an accident. In the record books he shows up as a good driver!

If you ever have to obstruct traffic because of illness or because your car is running poorly or for any other reason, remember to pull off the road now and then when safe and let everybody else get ahead. Signal your intentions well in advance. Be sure to choose a safe place, such as a wide gas-station driveway or a smooth shoulder where you can get off and back again without lurching. And maneuver smoothly in order not to endanger anyone.

The second car is often to blame. The real troublemaker when a slow driver is involved is often the second driver in line. This is the inattentive fellow, usually talking to a passenger, who dawdles behind the slow car and won't take advantage of safe opportunities he has to pass.

A slow driver alone rarely blocks more than two or three cars. That's because most drivers are alert enough to get around him when a safe passing zone appears.

But almost without exception, whenever a long line of cars builds up the real cause is the second driver. Since he won't use the passing zones,

Double Tailgaiting

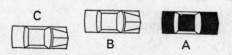

no one else can. Knowing this, the good driver does not dawdle when he finds himself second in line. He pulls ahead as soon as possible and in that way gives everybody else a chance.

HOW TO GET ALONG WITH TRUCK DRIVERS

Some friction now and then between motorists and truck drivers seems inevitable. One reason is size. Another reason is lack of communication. The truck driver thinks the motorist is holding him back, and the motorist thinks the truck driver is trying to bully him into going faster. Sometimes both are right.

Regardless of reasons, whenever you look in your mirror and see forty tons of truck following your bumper at 60 mph you're apt to get nervous. Sometimes you feel you can't escape; you just have to keep going as fast as you can. The skillful driver can sometimes go faster; but the inept driver may get in trouble if he or she tries.

Truck Drivers' Blind Spots

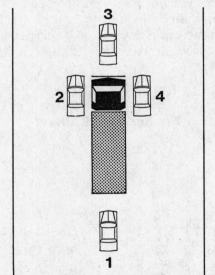

These are truck drivers' four worst "blind spots."

1. Behind-close.
2. Below his left elbow.
3. Directly ahead and below his windshield.
4. Below his right door.

On a busy road when all lanes are running full, you can't always get out of the way. And so many drivers run scared until the driver behind relents or squeezes into the next lane himself. Because of this some drivers who find such situations nerve-wracking desert the busy trucking highways for quieter routes, where they don't feel harassed.

However, your life among the trucks can be a lot easier if you know what the truck driver's own problems are. (And if you know how you look to him!)

It pays, too, to know what sort of accident situations the trucks get into so you can help truck drivers avoid them—and stay out of them yourself.

The first thing to know is that you look just as small to a truck driver as he looks big to you. In fact, in some big trucks the driver is seated so high and remote that when you're too close, he can't see you at all. This happens at traffic lights when some of the big fellows pull up close behind you. A car may actually be hidden below the truck's windshield frame or engine hood.

On the road remember that a truck driver is happy as long as he can keep an even speed. His troubles begin when he has to slow down or stop. We in our cars usually have three forward speeds. And when we stop or slow down, we can pick up speed quickly and easily. But a big truck may have twelve or more forward speeds without benefit of

The Busy Truck Driver

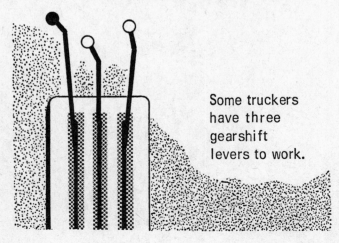

Some truckers have three gearshift levers to work.

an automatic transmission to help. When he has to stop—or go very slowly—he faces the necessity of "working up" through as many as ten gearshifts to return to regular road speed. This is a lot of hard work. At such times a truck driver at work in his cab looks as busy as an organist playing a Bach cantata. His arms are swinging, hands and feet flying. He gets a hard physical workout. It's small wonder he hates to stop or slow down behind you.

Meanwhile, here we are buzzing along in front or alongside, or behind him, speeding up, slowing down, changing lanes, holding him back. A wasp buzzing around his head would be less worrisome. And now and then some angry driver starts to harass him. Don't yield to this temptation; you're not only playing with his life—and yours. A car suddenly slowing down ahead may cause a fast truck to go slithering off the road in a deadly "jackknife." And the truck may sweep the offending car—or others—off the road with it.

There are good truck drivers and bad truck drivers. Many—especially those who work for big fleets on cross-country runs—are intelligent family men, trained in safety and as disciplined as pilots. Others have less discipline and less skill. If you find yourself near a truck whose driver seems annoyed, there's only one thing to do: Get away as soon and as safely as you can. Never argue with a truck. The driver may have a hot temper. And some, like many automobile drivers, may have been drinking. Give a truck driver all the road he wants and as soon as you can.

Other times to be careful:

1. *When being overtaken by fast trucks in snowstorms.* They can hold the road at high speed in deepening snow; you can't. Be careful you don't *spin* out of control in front of a truck. And when one overtakes you, slow down early and get ready for the bath of slush that blots out all windshield vision and even stalls your wiper blades.

2. *When tempted to overtake trucks in heavy rain.* (See "How's Your Passing?," page 49.)

3. *When overtaking on any straightaway.* Never run alongside a truck for more than a few seconds. Tires sometimes come apart, and locked airbrakes sometimes cause trucks to veer off the road. Further, the truck driver may have to change lanes and may not know you are there! If he starts to crowd in, don't rely on your horn for protection. Many truck cabs are so noisy that drivers can't even hear their own radios. Your horn goes unheard.

4. *When overtaking on a left curve (or being overtaken on a right*

Slush

Look out for the bath of slush that can stall your windshield wipers.

curve). Let's say you're approaching a slight left curve on an interstate highway. A truck is just ahead on your right.

For some reason some trucks tend to drift across the lane lines on high-speed curves. As the road begins to bank left for the curve, expect some trucks to creep over into your lane and crowd you. Don't be caught napping.

The situation reverses if you're in the right lane. The truck is just ahead on your left, and you're approaching a right curve. This time the truck may tend to stray from the left lane into your lane.

There is only one sure protection in either situation: Try never to run alongside trucks as you enter fast curves! Time your driving so that one of you will be well ahead as the curve begins.

5. *When caught in a cluster.* Get away—quickly—from any group of trucks trying to outmaneuver each other. When you spot two or three all going the same way, jockeying to overtake each other in tight quarters, put on speed or slow down, and stay out of the way. If something goes wrong in such a situation and the giants start to take emergency action among themselves, you may get run over.

Truck drivers now and then race each other—and this is another time to stay far away. However, when you see trucks jockeying for road space, they're not necessarily racing. Usually they're simply minding their own business. Like cars, trucks have their own best speed. Some go slightly faster, some slightly slower than others. As a rule slow trucks try to stay clear and help the fast ones get by; but in a tangle of traffic this may take several miles and it may seem to you that they're fighting. Usually it's just that each trucker is trying to hold his own best speed.

6. *When "dogged" by trucks on hills.* What can you do about the truck that plagues you by rushing down every hill at 60–65 mph, then slowing to 30 mph on the upslopes? If he's ahead, he blocks you. If he's behind, he may come rushing up to your rear bumper and scare you.

If you're blocked for long behind a truck on a hill-and-dale road, there's only one thing to do. Now and then, when it seems appropriate, flash your headlights quickly—just once or twice—day or night. He'll catch it. You're saying politely, "How about giving me a break when you get a chance?" Don't be insistent. Most truckers will watch for a wide shoulder or a special "climbing lane" into which they can pull to help you pass.

If you're ahead of such a truck and he keeps "rushing" close to your bumper on downgrades, you have two choices. Speed up (if safe) and leave him behind. Or in extreme danger turn on your hazard flashers. Flashing red lights always cry danger—and may persuade him to lay back a bit. (Running with hazard flashes is illegal in some states, however, as already noted.)

Even better, perhaps, you could wait for a safe chance, pull off the road, and let him get ahead. Obviously if the road ahead is so clogged with traffic that you can't outrun him, you have nothing to lose by falling in behind.

How To Help Trucks Turn Corners. Wheeling a big tractor-trailer around a sharp corner is a difficult job. Trucks need more turning room than cars.

You can help a truck by not pulling all the way up to the crosswalk when you stop for a red traffic light—if you see a truck approaching from either your left or your right. Stop about twenty feet back of the crosswalk to give him turning room.

Sometimes you will have stopped before you see the truck. In that case many drivers back up a few feet. This needs to be done with care. Pedestrians often cross in back of the first car stopped at a traffic light.

Whenever backing up is needed, it may be necessary to get the co-operation of the second and third cars behind you. They may have to back a few feet too.

MOTORCYCLES: WHERE TO WATCH FOR THEM

The proliferation of motorcycles and scooters has created new problems. The popular two-wheeled vehicles are so small and maneuverable that they sometimes appear in front of you (or beside you) with no

Cyclists

Expect cyclists to come toward you
when you are passing.

The small dot is a motorcyclist's head just
visible over a slight dip in the road in which a
car would be quite visible.

A motorcycle coming toward you while you are
overtaking another vehicle is very hard to see.

warning at all. To protect motorcycle and scooter riders and to save yourself from collision, it is now important to keep a special watch.

Don't change lanes to the right without actually turning your head to look for a "bike" rider in the blind zone that your mirror won't reach.

Don't change lanes to the left without checking both inside and outside mirrors—and remember that a motorcyclist's head bobbing behind your car can vanish from view for a second or two even while you are checking the mirrors.

Never ride close to motorcycles or scooters in traffic. Give them plenty of maneuvering room. And give them room to be seen by other drivers.

Be especially alert for oncoming motorcycles when pulling out to overtake other traffic on two-way roads. A motorcyclist coming toward you at a combined speed of 110 mph (your 55 plus his 55) is a very tiny object, indeed. In fact, on a hilly or "dipping" road he may simply be invisible until he is directly in front of you. This is one reason that all motorcycle riders should use daytime headlights when traveling on two-way roads. But unfortunately the practice is not yet uniform. Many bikes remain unlighted and hard to see.

Give motorcycles and scooters extra room whenever rain starts to fall. Skidding on wet pavement is a problem that afflicts many of them.

Give them extra room when you see them maneuvering on gravel or sand (as along the road's edge or when turning into gas stations where grit accumulates at the pavement edge). Many bike riders have taken sudden spills in small sandy patches even at speeds as slow as 15 mph, and if one spills in front of you, you may not avoid hitting him.

PART THREE

DRIVING UNDER
DANGEROUS CONDITIONS

CHAPTER XVIII

NIGHT DRIVING

NIGHT DRIVING IS three times as dangerous as day driving, according to the National Safety Council. If you ask anyone why, you will get an interesting variety of reasons.

But experts are now beginning to believe that intoxication is mainly involved. At night many of the drivers you pass have been drinking.

The great troublemaker at night, as previously noted, is not the mild social drinker but the "super-drunk," who gets out of control and suddenly comes toward you, head-on, on your side. Sometimes, however, he rams your car from behind. In blind intoxication he does not see your taillights.

So you need to take special precautions at night. Always keep watch for any car that appears to be weaving or acting strangely. Never stop at a highway traffic light without keeping watch behind you for any car that appears to be coming very fast.

Watching Headlights

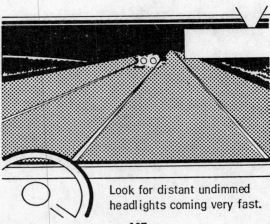

Look for distant undimmed headlights coming very fast.

Other than by his wrong-way or excessively fast driving, the best way to spot a badly intoxicated driver at night is by his undimmed headlights. (See also Chapter XVII.) Be on guard against any car whose driver fails to lower his lights either when approaching from ahead or overtaking from behind. Give such a car extra room and be on the alert for erratic steering or failure to brake.

You can greatly cut the odds in favor of a night collision merely by staying off certain roads at certain hours. A California Division of Highways study shows that the "super-drunk" usually comes out at bar-closing time. He threatens havoc for the next hour. This is the driver who causes most grim head-on collisions that wipe out several lives.

Other pointers for night driving:

Allow for the fact that some oncoming cars are nearer than they look. That's because headlights on some cars (especially small ones) are close together. Close headlights can make a sportscar two hundred feet away look as if it's a quarter-mile off.

Contrary to what you may think, you see very little at night, because there simply are no "powerful headlights." Headlights that seem so bright are really quite weak. (If sunlight were as weak, you'd find it hard to read a newspaper.) For this reason you should never relax in night driving. Make your eyes search out every possible detail. Make extra allowance for heavily tinted windshields, which reduce vision— even in early dusk—and shun the sunglasses that some drivers wear at night. Never squint at oncoming lights. This blots out needed detail.

How to meet glaring lights. Don't anchor your eyes to the right edge

Headlight Glare

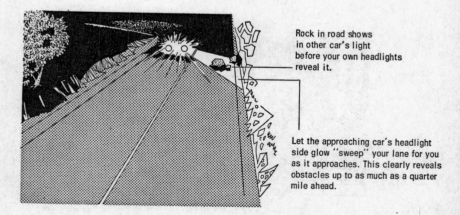

Rock in road shows in other car's light before your own headlights reveal it.

Let the approaching car's headlight side glow "sweep" your lane for you as it approaches. This clearly reveals obstacles up to as much as a quarter mile ahead.

Smooth and Bumpy Roads

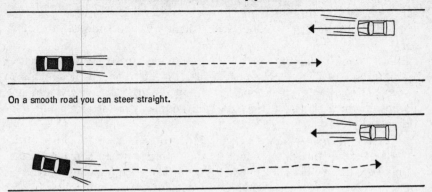

On a smooth road you can steer straight.

On a bumpy road your car not only bounces but veers from side to side.

of the road—or you may not see a pedestrian crossing from the left. Don't focus on any fixed spot. Instead, try roving your eyes constantly in a triangle pattern: (1) to the right edge just ahead, (2) to a point in your lane just beside the approaching car, and then (3) to the center lane at a point halfway to the approaching car. Then start all over again. Look No. 1 sets your course, helps you steer. Look No. 2 employs the other car's lights to "sweep" the road for you as they approach. (Most cars cast a side ray into your lane.) And Look No. 3 lets you detect instantly any slight waver in the approaching car's line of travel. It makes the center line your measuring stick for safe passing. It's your protection against a drunk.

But Look No. 3 serves another purpose: It will reveal to you, outlined by the other car's lights, any bumps, holes, debris, pedestrians, and a host of small details that may not be seen if you look only at the edge.

The moment of truth. For some drivers on narrow roads there's always a last, scary second before they meet and pass. In the last seconds their car may lurch uncertainly, feel its way, and drop a wheel off the road's edge. The driver never really knows whether he is going to plow into a parked truck during the "moment of blindness."

All this is quite needless.

On a smooth road. When the pavement is smooth you can virtually stop worrying about the "moment of blindness" if you have made proper use of Look No. 2. If you have let the other driver's approaching headlights sweep your side of the road for you, you know that your lane now is clear for the distance you have watched his light on your lane.

You now know that there is no pedestrian walking on the road, no stalled car, no holes, puddles, or bumps.

In spite of this, always reduce speed slightly as you approach the other car.

On a rough road. But on a rough, "bouncy" road, you have a different problem. Here, too, you can use the approaching headlights to sweep the road. But you should slow down sharply because lumps and bumps in the last critical seconds can change your steering aim considerably.

Use low beams on sharp curves. Many drivers go into blind curves on high beams ("brights"), and then get startled when someone comes around a curve without warning. It is a mistake to approach blind curves on high beam only since your brights blot out the advance glare of cars coming toward you. We're speaking, of course, of those sharp curves which normally are taken at speeds below 45 mph.

Entering any blind turn at night it is good practice to switch to low beams at least momentarily. If another car is coming, you will be able to see its headlight glow clearly as soon as you drop your beams.

But also use a warning "flick." Sometimes it is quite safe to stay on low beam during the entire curve. But if you do, it also pays to flick to brights once or twice just for a second. This sends a flash of light around the apex of the curve and helps the other driver know you are coming.

Look for "deer lights." One of the worst problems at night is deer. Countless motorists have hit them or have had a close brush. (The author has hit one, has seen another nearly cause a wreck involving five cars, and has even watched a big doe jump over the hood of his car as he turned into a farm road.) Hitting a deer at any speed over 45 mph can be serious. It has killed many drivers.

Keep a sharp watch for deer on any rural road, especially toward dawn. That is when deer come out of woods and fields to feed in roadside ditches. The thing to look for is not the deer itself but *deer's eyes.* Deer are virtually invisible, but a deer's eye shines like a cat's. It looks like a small pocket flashlight moving near the road or like the shiny end of a soft-drink can hung in bushes or trees. One way to know when you are seeing deer is when you see only one eye. You may see two cat's eyes at night or two dog's eyes, but a deer watches you with the side of its face, and generally only one eye reflects your headlights.

When you see deer, brake fast, for a deer won't turn like a cat and run back into the woods; he usually jumps directly into the road and if he pauses there for even an instant, you may not be able to get around him.

When you see one deer, always look for others. One deer leaping across a road is often followed by a second and sometimes by a whole procession. And they rarely turn back. If the leader goes, they will all follow, even though they run right into your car.

Should you use high beams on a superhighway? This is hard to answer even for the experts. Unfortunately most of our newest roads are designed so that you simply cannot use your brights at all. Other cars are always in sight on the other track. And if you use high beams, you throw a glare at other drivers. Because of this, many drivers have been advised to *"use low beams on interstate roads but don't overdrive them!"*

Taken seriously, this would slow night traffic on all super-roads to about 40 mph or less, for many low-beam headlights shine no more than one hundred feet ahead. And the minimum legal speed on many super-highways is 45 mph.

Obviously drivers are not going to slow to 40 mph on a long night trip on a splendid highway. Yet at 55 mph low beams will never reveal trouble ahead (for example, a confused pedestrian in the road, fallen cargo from a truck, or a heavy tire recap thrown off a wheel). To hit any of these can be disaster.

And so what *can* you do?

Reflection Driving. You can learn a whole new technique: driving by reflection. Cease to rely solely on your headlights. Train your eyes by constant practice and close observation to see by other means. For example:

1. *Steer by other car lights.* Cars proceeding ahead of you cast a good deal of side glow. Watch closely and see how well they can sweep the road for you.

2. *Read the reflector posts.* These on many roads form a brilliant corridor of light against which a stalled car or truck will show up black.

3. *Read the road striping* (edge stripes and lane stripes) as far ahead as possible. Debris, dogs, even pedestrians show up as black gaps in the stripe.

4. *Read the reflection of oncoming lights.* There is an astonishing amount of reflection on most dry roads, either blacktop or concrete. And watch for the night mirage effect—"puddles" of reflected headlights against which any obstruction in the road will show up sharply.

5. *Let taillights help.* The taillights of other cars show lane stripes and bumps—sometimes before your own lights pick them up.

What to do if your headlights go out. It isn't common, but when it *does* happen, it is an experience no driver will ever forget.

If your lights fail on a busy road, other cars' lights will help delineate the road for you, and your main problem may be to get parked on the shoulder before your car gets hit. On a deserted road, however, you may have a more serious problem. The entire roadway may vanish.

Here is what you can do:

1. Get your four-way hazard flashers on (or your left-turn signal) *quickly*. If there is a center line, some flashers will pick it out dimly in a series of flashes and guide you to a stop.

2. If there is no center line, hunt for the right edge with the hazard flashers or your right turn signal.

3. If all your lights go out, including even the turn signals, lighted signs, houses, or buildings sometimes cast faint reflections in the road. If there is no light at all, it may be best to hold the wheel centered and stop fast in a series of quick brake "stabs." (See also "The Panic Stop," page 22.) Don't lock wheels and skid. Don't turn the wheel unless you were approaching a turn when the lights failed.

4. If your lights suddenly come on, proceed with great caution because they usually go off again! If lights reappear, never assume that "the trouble is fixed" and resume speed. Always have a mechanic find and repair the trouble. Lighting trouble never "fixes itself"; it is still there.

5. In dire emergency, as when you have stopped on the pavement and will get hit from behind if you stay there, you may want to have a passenger with a flashlight get out on the safe side and lead you to safety on the shoulder. But this is only a "last resort" procedure. It is highly dangerous to you both and is justified only when it is the "lesser danger." Remember that other drivers may not see his flashlight. (See Chapter XX.)

6. On deserted roads in critical emergency, remember that you can also run backward a short distance by using your backup lights—if not affected by the failure. This can enable you to find a safe place on the shoulder or turn safely into a driveway or small side road. To attempt to back against moving traffic with backup lights, however, is sure invitation to disaster.

Above all, if the lights fail, never under any circumstances assume that other drivers can see your darkened car. They cannot. Leave the inside dome light on—if it still works. It's dim, but it helps. Hang reflective material on back of the car. Light a small bonfire if safe. Do everything possible to be seen. Get the car to a safe place. And make sure that in taking these precautions no one gets hit!

CHAPTER XIX

RAIN, FOG, AND DANGEROUS STORMS

RAIN AND "PATH OF LIGHT" DRIVING

WHEN RAIN STARTS TO FALL, emergency tow-truck drivers always get ready. So do the police, who know that within minutes their switchboards will be lighting up with emergency calls.

Yet it is astonishingly easy not to have trouble in rain. Here are some useful tips:

Use windshield washers when light drizzle starts. Otherwise your wiper blades may turn the first few drops into an oily smear. This makes visibility difficult in the daytime and almost impossible at night.

Turn on lights. In rain cars tend to disappear. Use parking lights, at least, to make your car more visible. If rain increases, use day headlights (low beam).

Turn on blower. Rain usually comes with high humidity, causing windshields and windows to fog up. Put your defroster blower to work on the windshield.

Or use your air conditioner, if you have one. This quickly clears inside fog off the windshield—and windows too.

Crank up windows to keep from getting splashed! Other cars, running through puddles, sometimes send a spray of muddy water in through open windows. This often hits drivers in the face.

Look out for the oily road slick that forms in new rain. During the first thirty minutes of light rain, oil and dust on street pavements change to a slippery substance that is as slick as ice. Tires skid very easily.

Watch for running pedestrians. In heavy showers pedestrians pull coats or newspapers over their heads and run. They don't see you. And since heavy rain also makes a good deal of noise, they don't hear you coming.

At night drive with a "rain foot"—one that is ready instantly to lift off the gas pedal. In rain you may not see cars until the last minute—especially cars in side streets.

Let's take a closer look at these problems and the best ways to cope with them when you're driving on the open highway.

A lifesaver on rainy nights: "path-of-light" driving. A new technique that the author calls "path-of-light" driving makes car-handling on wet nights much easier and safer.

Briefly, it consists of steering by the reflections that suddenly appear in the road when rain wets the pavement. Many drivers overlook the usefulness of such reflections. Yet they can be made to reveal clearly any turns, any chuckholes, and even pedestrians.

The eye must be trained to "read" every possible reflection. These come from approaching headlights, street lights, lighted or reflectorized signs, even farmhouse windows by a dark country road ahead. The amount of useful illumination cast by such lights is quite phenomenal.

Approaching headlights often cast a path of reflected light several hundred feet long. A single street light at a corner far ahead can lay down a brilliant and helpful path of illumination *a half mile long.* A large reflectorized sign will also light a long useful path. Even a wet curbstone can provide a brilliant guidance line for two or three blocks through the confusion of traffic on city streets at night. This "curbstone light path" doesn't come from your own headlights at all: it is "bounced" to you from the headlights of approaching cars. It will reveal parked cars, pedestrians about to start across a street, even dogs and small children.

This technique is so useful on rainy nights that the author has recommended to engineers that it be considered in the designing of highways and streets. Tests made with New York University's Professor William J. Toth showed that when there were no reflections in the pavement pupils crossing a certain school street on a rainy night became totally invisible. Not even the test car's headlights revealed them. But when a light was turned on in a distant store window, the pupils were clearly seen. Their figures were silhouetted against the long path of reflection—even though the light which provided it was more than a block beyond them.

The rear visibility gap and what to do about it. The rear windows of some cars (and especially station wagons) become heavily coated with rain and dirt. When this happens, drivers cannot see behind them.

In a recent road test it was demonstrated that a driver in daylight could not see *any* of three vehicles traveling close behind in three lanes. During moderate to heavy rains they simply vanished behind his spattered rear window.

But in the same test when one of the three following cars lighted its parking lights or headlights, its presence immediately became known inside the test car ahead. The lights cut through the spattered glass. They created a bright yellow glare in its rainswept rear window and shone in the mirror. The car itself could not be seen from the test car but its lights could!

The importance of good tires. If your tires are fairly new and fresh, with good, thick treads, cut your speed slightly in rain. But if treads are showing a bit of wear, reduce speed *sharply*. Worn or nearly bald tires generally have good stopping power on dry roads. But the converse holds true on wet roads: A worn-out tread or a bald tire (now illegal in some states) may have no grip at all. It simply slides.

Adjust speed to rain and road surface. In light rain, if the legal speed on a superhighway is 55 mph, an expert with good tires might drop his speed to 50 during the first half-hour until the slippery oil film has been scrubbed away by tires. After that he might go back up to a careful 53. If he goes to 55, he will do so with great caution.

In heavy rain cut speed even more. Drop speed to 40–45 or, in extremely heavy rain, even less.

Beware a "dimpled" road! When a heavy shower falls and "dimples" appear in the road, tires start to ride on top of the rain. This hydroplan-

Hydroplaning

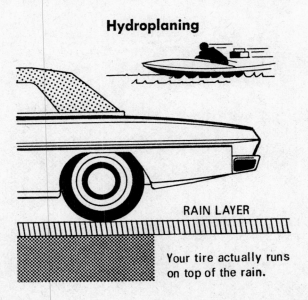

RAIN LAYER

Your tire actually runs on top of the rain.

ing effect was discovered by engineers of the National Aeronautics and Space Administration (NASA). It begins at 35 mph and gets worse above that speed. A hydroplaning tire at 60 mph in deep rain becomes a boat and loses all ability to grip the road. It can't turn safely or stop safely because it simply has no traction at all.

NASA scientists also found that "rain dimples" are the best visual warning you can get. They begin to appear when the water becomes deep enough (quarter-inch) to cause hydroplaning.

Don't hit puddles at high speed. Puddles not only cause hydroplaning but can pull your car around out of control. No good driver will overtake another vehicle if he sees big puddles.

Choose the driest lane. The right lane gets more traffic than the others and generally is the driest.

Drive the "tire wipes." "Wipes" are the tracks left by moving cars whose tires have wiped the road almost dry. Tires tend to float and lose control—at high speed especially—when a lane is covered by a quarter-inch or more of water. Driving the wipes gives your tires a firmer grip. (You *don't* have to tailgate the car ahead in order to use his wipes, however. His tracks will stay fairly dry for at least one-tenth of a mile, even in heavy rain.)

"Tire Wipes"

Don't overtake through a "spray curtain" on narrow roads. A fast car (and especially a fast truck) ahead of you throws a large curtain of spray when rain is heavy.

It is bad practice to overtake another fast vehicle on a two-way road when its spray hides your view. Besides loss of vision there is a further serious problem. Just as your car tries to enter the spray curtain, it may be buffeted by a shock wind that the other vehicle generates. In the case of a fast truck this wind can be very strong. To control a car on a slippery road when blind and buffeted by side wind is difficult. Let the truck stay ahead until it reduces speed.

Drive as though you had no brakes—because you may not! Puddles sometimes soak brakes and make them useless. After going through deep water, proceed cautiously (if safe), applying brakes *frequently* until they dry out.

"A road is as slick as it looks." Trust your eyes to judge how slippery a wet road is. A road full of smooth reflections that *looks* slippery usually is! The men who test cars in skids have found that a wet road, especially wet blacktop, is almost as slippery as ice.

Yellow filters help. For a daytime trip in rain it may help to purchase one of the bright yellow filters that skiers wear over their eyes. Many ordinary sunglasses are a handicap in rain because they darken the view. But the author has found a yellow ski filter of great help. It can be worn with or without glasses and it actually brightens distant objects on rainy days. Even more important, it cuts through the glare caused by raindrops falling on a windshield. Thus the blurred windshield ceases to obscure the road, which in daylight shows up far more clearly.

The yellow filter does not seem to offer this advantage at night; in fact, it lowers visibility slightly.

FOG

One spring day in a Southern state, a small truck stopped in dense fog made worse by industrial smoke. A woman approaching at slow speed hit the truck before she could see it. Then a second car hit hers, and that in turn was hit by a third car. Soon sixteen wrecks were strung along the road in one huge pileup.

The worst was still to come.

Rumbling up from Florida was a big fruit truck. Because of the fog its driver was in the wreckage before he knew it. The truck rode on top of one car, crushing it with three persons inside. It pushed the car,

Fog-Caused Chain Collision

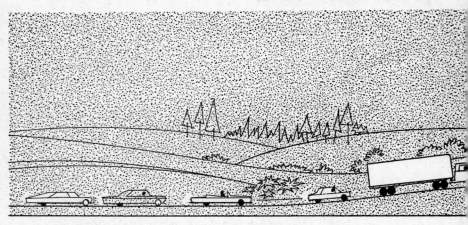

A chain collision in the making. Everyone is blindly following the taillight ahead.

screeching on concrete, into other cars. A fuel tank burst. Soon all six lanes were blocked by flaming cars. The highway was closed for hours. Sixteen people lay hurt. Three died.

Such fog chain collisions never used to be much of a hazard. But higher speeds have changed that. Often drivers form in lines behind some leader who is foolish enough to blaze a trail at high speed. Yet such a leader may be steering by nothing more than a road stripe which disappears perhaps fifty feet (two and a half car lengths) ahead of him. If he hits something, everyone else will hit together. This has caused pileups of as many as a hundred cars. The possibilities for disaster in fog are enormous.

What, then, can you do to protect yourself?

Get off any high-speed expressway or freeway as quickly as possible when thick fog forms. You'll be a lot safer from rear-end collision on lesser roads.

Turn on your wipers. Much "dense fog" that bothers drivers is merely a fine accumulation of mist on the windshield! You can't see it against the fog, so you never suspect it is there. But when your wipers start, fog often proves to be not nearly so dense as you thought it was.

Turn on taillights even in day fog. Without them your car is invisible to anyone coming behind you at high speed.

Don't rely on front parking lights. Turn on low-beam headlights in day fog. Parking lights are weak and often invisible. You need headlights to ward off a head-on collision with any car coming toward you

in the Making

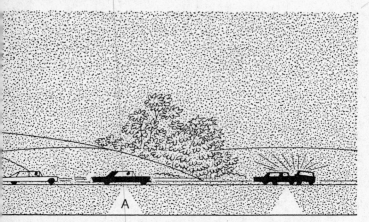

Car A is leading them all into the wreck.   ACCIDENT

in your lane while passing a slower car. Your headlights in fog are often seen several seconds before your car itself. If you have no headlights, the approaching driver may not see you until too late to pull back. Even on a divided highway day headlights will warn anyone who may be standing in the road after an accident—or any driver ahead of you who is thinking of stopping.

No expert driver will ever be lured into joining a "high-speed chain" in fog. He knows that the leader could be three miles ahead, reckless, sleepy, or intoxicated. Don't join a chain with the false idea that if anything goes wrong, somebody ahead of you will get hit first and you will have time to escape the collision! You won't. And what's worse, you won't be able to stop all those other cars in the chain who are now rushing blindly toward your rear bumper!

It's usually safe, however, to join a low-speed chain, especially if you're in the middle of it. Now you're moderately protected fore and aft. It sometimes makes good sense to follow the taillights of a car that is proceeding sensibly at very cautious speed. What is cautious speed? Here's a rule of thumb:

If you can see six car lengths ahead and no more: possibly 20–30 mph maximum.

If you can see two car lengths and no more: possibly 10–15 mph.

If you're running alone or are last man in a slow chain, take extra care to protect the rear of your car against some fast comer.

To do this some drivers use four-way flashers while running. (This

is an excellent idea but is forbidden in some states. Check your laws.)
Flashers will help supplement your taillights. If you have no four-way
flashers, use of a flashing turn signal might be considered in an emergency. The flashing gets attention. But keep a constant sharp watch in
your mirror. If another car now appears behind you, you know that he
has seen you and you should now cancel the signal temporarily—in
order not to lead him to think that you are really planning to turn.

The two fog emergencies most likely to happen are these:

Emergency Situation No. 1: Fog gets so thick that you can't see the
road's edge—or anything else to guide you.

In this case the only sensible thing usually is to find the right edge,
pull far off on a safe shoulder, stop—and wait for the fog to go away.

But often there is no shoulder and sometimes we're compelled to keep
going even when we shouldn't.

If you're alone and "struggling on," here are some tricks that sometimes help. If your headlights hopelessly blind you at night, use your
left-turn light. Its yellow flashing will sometimes show a road stripe.
From this you can determine where the shoulder is.

Flicking your lights to high beam briefly and then repeating the flick
once every few yards will pick out roadside post reflectors that would
never show up for your low beams.

Emergency Situation No. 2: In dense fog you have a minor collision,
engine failure, or flat tire and stall in a heavily traveled lane. Or you may
be blocked by a wreck. There's no shoulder or, if there is, you cannot
reach it for safety.

Driving

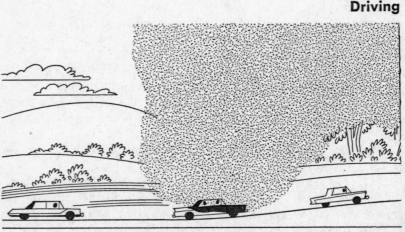

This driver is almost totally blind   Fog lifts here.
in dense, low patch.

What to do. Seconds count. To protect other motorists flame flares must immediately be run out some distance behind you. This is a dangerous operation! Be careful not to be run down. And if you're on a two-way road, flares may also be needed in the opposite direction. Meanwhile, everyone in the affected car should be moved to a safe place well off the road.

When venturing into fog it is wise to have three or more flame flares within instant reach—not locked in the trunk.

If on a two-way road, place one flare where it can be seen from both directions. At once light a second one (see flare procedure, pages 158–159) and hurry it back. Walk along the edge, never in the road. In fog plant the flare at the edge, seventy-five paces back (roughly two hundred feet). If cars are moving, don't wait until you get there to light it. Light a thirty-minute flare and walk it back another one hundred paces. You now have one warning nearly five hundred feet back, which is a minimum even in fog.

Why do some drivers go so fast in fog? Truck drivers sit much higher than you. They actually look down on your car's roof. They are often above the thick ground fog that causes trouble for car drivers. Furthermore, a truck driver looks down through his headlight beams; hence he is less apt to be blinded by back glare and can see a bit farther than you.

This induces him to move faster. The big fleet drivers, carefully trained by safety experts, are not apt to overdo their fog speed. But unfortunately some untrained truck drivers are lured into trying foolish fog

in Fog

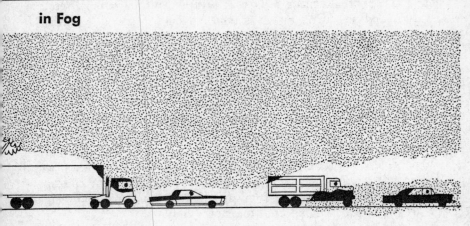

Truckdriver can't see here, but sportscar driver can see under this patch.

Truckdriver can see over low ground fog here. Car driver is blind.

speeds of 50 and even 60 mph. And at such speeds it may take a truck at least one-tenth of a mile to stop.

Car drivers who speed through fog simply don't realize the danger. Some motorists and truckers fancy themselves "good fog drivers." Now and then they glimpse a road stripe or a post, and so they race through fog guided only by these occasional glimpses. Experts know there is no such thing as a "good fog driver."

One final note:

You can usually escape from fog—if you act immediately. The trick is to turn around where possible and go back! Fog does not usually descend everywhere all at once. It has a *shape,* like a cloud. It forms and advances slowly. When you run into it, if you turn around quickly, you can usually run out again the way you came in. This isn't always true. But even when fog is developing over a wide area, there are usually thin areas into which you can retreat—to find a safe refuge.

Turning around on superhighways, of course, is impossible except at an interchange. If none is at hand, your best refuge may be a service area or a place on a wide shoulder many feet from the road. Try never to keep going on a high-speed road when fog really gets thick.

Do yellow lights (or sunglasses) really help?

Some drivers use special yellow (amber) lights for driving in fog. Often these are small supplementary lamps mounted lower than the headlights, and they're supposed to penetrate the fog close to the road. Do they? No one knows for sure. Some drivers think they are a great help; others believe this is imaginary. Some do seem to have value.

But there is no doubt that some sunglasses do help cut fog in daylight. The author has made tests with several pairs of rather average sunglasses and has found that it is quite possible to see a bit farther, at least under some conditions. Also of use are the special yellow snowglasses that skiers use.

DANGEROUS STORMS

Rain is bad enough, but when accompanied by wind and lightning on a superhighway, it can be extremely hazardous. Here's what to do if you get trapped in a bad thunderstorm.

If possible, stop driving until the storm passes. Choose a safe place, away from traffic, trees, tall poles, and wires. A steep earth embankment often offers good shelter from the wind. If you can't stop, here's how to adjust your driving until the storm ends.

Lightning

Lightning won't hurt you in your car, but it can scare and dazzle you.

Lightning is no direct danger to you inside your car. However, bolts striking very close to you can blind or startle you, so lower your speed when lightning starts to flash.

Wind. Gusts can confuse you and force you to stop at a spot where you may be hit by other confused drivers. When you see clouds of dust coming—a sign that wind is about to hit—pull off in a safe place and stop before the wind arrives.

When wind hits, look out for flying branches.

In a strong wind be alert for fallen wires. If your car body itself becomes entangled in live wires that are still sparking or smoking, stay in the car and wait until someone tells you that power has been cut off. Your rubber tires protect you in a car on which a live wire has fallen. But putting one foot to the ground can electrocute you.

Hail is a sign of great turbulence in clouds and may signal a far more violent squall of wind and rain still to come.

Heavy Rain

Look out for flooded underpasses.

Heavy Rain. Beware of sudden freshets (especially in areas where flash floods are common). If you seek shelter in a "dip" under a bridge, be sure to move on when water begins to accumulate. Many drivers get trapped in deep water when storm drains under bridges become clogged. Stalled cars in underpass floods sometimes are completely submerged. Don't run fast through puddles and be careful in deep water not to go fast enough to cause it to drown your engine. Proceed at a crawl.

Tornadoes. According to the Weather Bureau, some tornadoes (or "funnel clouds") move by themselves; others are hidden inside severe thunderstorms that drop large hail. Tornadoes often show up first as strange green-black or purple spots in the clouds. Intense, continuous lightning flashing in one pocket of clouds also can indicate the presence of a tornado.

Another tip: When tornado funnels are hidden in thunderstorms, they often conceal themselves in the southwest corner of the storm. Thus if driving west or south in a bad storm during a tornado alert, look for a twister near the end of the storm. If driving east or north, beware of any unusually black, purplish or green clouds near the rear of any storm you are overtaking.

Tornadoes with or without thunderstorms usually travel northeast at speeds of 25 to 40 miles an hour. If a tornado follows you, you can easily outrun it, but only if there is no traffic jam ahead.

If trapped by the great violence of an approaching tornado and there is time to leave your car, you may find shelter behind large rocks, in ditches or small culverts, or even under the bridges that span superhighways. Stay away from trees. They fall and crush cars.

Remember: You need protection not only from wind but from the pulverizing shrapnel of stone, dirt, broken glass, and wood that whirls in tornadoes at explosive speed.

If you cannot leave your car, lock the doors, crank up windows tight, but open one on the side away from the wind, just an inch or two. Then lie on the floor. Cover your head and face with coats, cushions, luggage. Drivers trapped in tornadoes have survived by lying with their heads under the dashboard, against the engine firewall.

Special advice for travelers: In severe weather keep your radio on. If you ever hear a warning that a tornado is actually moving toward a town in which you have stopped, don't delay. If you cannot find an underground storm shelter handy, get in your car and take the best escape route away from the tornado immediately. Drivers who "wait to see" get caught in jams of escaping cars.

Escaping by car is far better than seeking shelter in any above-ground building in the path of an approaching tornado.

How to "Outwit" a Bad Thunderstorm. When a storm approaches, it usually gives warning: dark clouds by day and lightning by night. Radio weather forecasts also warn of approaching storms. A rapid crackling on your car radio may also be a signal that a storm is moving somewhere nearby—probably not over twenty to thirty miles away.

When you know that a bad storm is coming, there are three things you can do:

1. Just before it begins, stop in a comfortable place, safe from traffic, and wait for it to go through.
2. Turn and run away from it! This is amazingly easy to do.
3. Go around it.

The first thing every driver should know about individual thunderstorms is that as a rule they aren't very big. Thunderstorms are rarely larger than ten miles in diameter, and many are only a mile or two wide. Thus they are easy to dodge—if you spot them and know which way they are moving. Many move on a schedule of sorts. There are, for example, the notorious "four-o'clock squalls" that hit Washington, D.C., the Chesapeake Bay area, upstate New York, and parts of the Midwest and South. These often climax hot, sticky afternoons.

Most storms move with an advancing cold front, a wave of cool wind coming down from northwest or north. Keep tab by listening to hourly forecasts.

In general the really violent thunderstorms that you want to avoid move from west to east.

When a cold wind is moving down into a hot, sticky region, it usually pushes down from the northwest. But the thunderstorms that it breeds form on its leading edge and are pushed generally eastward, as the diagram shows.

Because of this:

Northbound cars should beware of black clouds (or intense pockets of lightning) ahead—or ahead and slightly to the left. A thunderstorm there will usually move across your route. It may pay you to stop now for a snack, let it move past, and then continue north.

Southbound cars should beware of thunderstorms seen ahead or ahead and to the right. These may be expected to cross your route. This, too, is a good time to stop in a comfortable place and wait. (Few thunderstorms last longer than thirty minutes.)

Westbound cars should be on guard against vicious black thunderstorms that appear directly ahead or ahead and slightly to the right. Here you will be bucking wind and rain head-on. Because of this, your own speed—even though you are going very slowly—will make the storm seem much worse than it is—and more blinding. There is danger on high-speed roads of hitting or being hit by other vehicles. Blinding rain erases all visibility; windshield wipers can't cope with it.

On an ordinary road: Stop in a safe place. Or if the thunderstorm looks violent, turn and go back a few miles. Then stop and wait and see if it won't move north (or south) of you. You can tell by watching the sky.

On a superhighway: Wait in a service area. Don't risk getting caught in fast-travel lanes.

(Note: Sometimes it is quite possible to steer entirely around a thunderstorm. If you see that a black-looking storm is quite small, it is quite possible to take a side road north (or south) for a few miles, then turn

Avoiding Thunderstorms

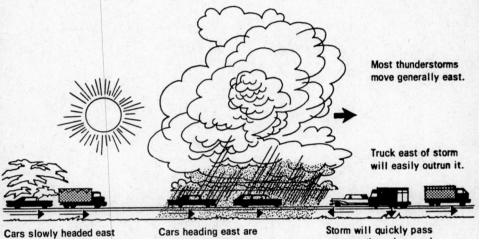

Most thunderstorms move generally east.

Truck east of storm will easily outrun it.

Cars slowly headed east a mile or two behind storm may even have bright, sunny weather all the way.

Cars heading east are stuck inside dangerous storm, at slow speed, and may be inside it for many miles.

Storm will quickly pass over westbound car and truck parked on shoulder to wait it out.

west, pass around one side of the storm, and return shortly to your route.)

Eastbound cars have an advantage. They are usually moving in the same direction as thunderstorms. Hence if you see a storm behind you, you can simply outrun it, because few thunderstorms travel faster than 25 mph.

But if you see black clouds, severe lightning, and evidence of high winds ahead, then you are overtaking a thunderstorm. Slow down and let it stay ahead until it wanders off your route or dissipates. If you do overtake it and find it too severe, you need only stop in a safe place for a few minutes. The storm, still moving east, will run away from you.

CHAPTER XX

WINTER DRIVING

HOW TO GO IN SNOW

When snow lies deep, many drivers get stuck unnecessarily. Usually the trouble is caused by fundamental errors in car handling.

Drivers make the following mistakes:

They park in positions from which they cannot escape in snow.

They go too fast—or too slow!

They don't use tires that will take a good "bite" on the snow.

They stop when they should keep moving.

They let their wheels spin.

The tips that follow include some practical driving "tricks" used by professionals, but it should be remembered that tricky driving is always attended by danger. So employ all tricks with good sense and only when needed.

Warning: A *bad* snowstorm is a far more serious problem than most drivers realize. Never venture into one if you can help it. Even the expert should stay off the roads when the forecast is for heavy snow or blizzard. Only a driver who has been caught in a blizzard knows its overwhelming power. In a blizzard—heavy snow with frigid winds over 40 mph—the simple truth is: No car or truck or bus can keep going very long. A stall is inevitable—and perhaps a real danger as well to people stranded in your car. The only sensible procedure is to seek warm shelter before the inevitable strikes and you find yourself stuck.

The following pointers are for ordinary (nonblizzard) snowstorms:

If you have to "buck" through a deep drift (or through the deep ridge of snow cast by a plow), always stop immediately afterward to check your radiator. After such impact, snow sometimes plugs radiators, causes engines to overheat. If you open the hood and find snow wedged in your radiator, stop your engine and remove what you can. Don't attempt to drive. If you cannot reach all the snow, it will help to let your car stand a while with engine stopped. Or if the day is very cold, let the engine idle—so long as it does not boil. The engine's heat will gradually melt snow that would not melt in a moving car. Resume driving only when it is all gone.

Here are some good winter rules:

1. *Never wait for a storm to hit.* When a storm is forecast, a good snow driver parks his car in such a manner and place that he will be able to move it afterward. He avoids tight parking spots where his car may be sealed in by passing plows. And he parks inches farther from the curb than usual, because he knows that wheels spin and cars get stuck when tires rub against curbstones in deep snow.

He avoids parking on slopes where he will have to start uphill later. Instead, he parks downhill and, if possible, with a clear space ahead in order to assure himself an easy downhill start.

He does not run his car into the garage head-on at night. Instead, he backs in. With at least fifteen feet of dry concrete next morning, his wheels will be able to give him a much better start in deep snow. And he won't have to turn around, which causes stalls.

Snow Driving

Don't park uphill.

Park downhill.

He will have trouble backing out.

He will get out and get a good start because he backed into the garage last night.

Studded tires take
a good bite on snow.

2. *Always use snow tires.* It is futile to try to go very far through deep snow without the right tires. These include snow treads, studded tires, and certain "radial" tires that work well in some kinds of snow. Some ordinary tires with thick treads will do a fairly good job for a while when new. But they may spin uselessly on the first hill. Some communities issue tickets to drivers of cars that are not equipped with snow tires on designated thoroughfares.

3. *Keep an open track.* When a storm begins, it helps to run in and out of a driveway every hour or two to keep a track open. If it happens to be an overnight storm, make a track just before you go to bed and again first thing in the morning, before your breakfast. Fresh snow is loose and easy to move. But the longer it stands the heavier and harder it gets.

If, for example, you wish to buck a track through piled snow left to block your driveway by a passing plow, don't wait several hours to do so. Go out at once and drive through it (if safe). Piled snow may later become almost as hard as concrete.

4. *Put "snow weight" in the rear.* The most common cause of snow stalls today is something few drivers think about: lack of enough weight over the driving wheels. The rear of an ordinary car is so light that tires—even snow tires—often fail to dig in and push. (A front-wheel-drive car, of course, is an exception. So too are certain small cars whose clean undersides offer little resistance and do not have to be pushed through deep snow.)

Many experienced professionals place extra snow weight in back, over—or slightly behind—the rear wheels. This adds traction. The wheels now can do their work, push the car, and help to keep it from skidding. Highway maintenance engineers in Colorado's beautiful Rocky Mountains never go out without at least one hundred pounds of sandbags over their rear wheels. (Some use three hundred pounds.) These are skilled drivers who have to get through. And they fight some of the heaviest snowfalls in the world. Even test drivers for the Goodyear Company add weight in winter.

For the average driver in, say, a foot to eighteen inches of snow, transferring passengers to the back seat may be all the extra snow weight that's needed. Even keeping a full gas tank helps weight the rear. If you use sandbags, be sure to use dry sand. Wet sand freezes rock-hard. In case of collision, the frozen bag could come through the back seat and hit you.

Caution: Adding a moderate amount of weight over the rear wheels naturally changes the balance of your car slightly. This must be taken into account sensibly in driving. The effect, however, is not great. It is roughly the same as loading the family car for a vacation with people, pets, and baggage in back plus a full tank of gas. The car doesn't steer quite so quickly. And if you should go into a skid, the rear end may tend to "spin out" faster, causing loss of control.

Snow: Wheel Loading

NO. This car (light in the rear) will get stuck.

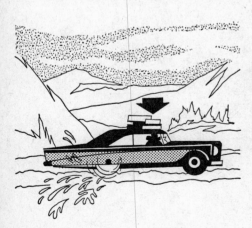

YES. This car is temporarily off balance but will go better through deep, untrodden snow.

But do not let this deter you from adding "rear-wheel weight" if you drive sensibly. For the fact is that any car without sufficient weight on its rear wheels to provide traction is a peril on any highway today— especially on any fast superhighway. It is a far greater peril than a car moderately weighted and sensibly driven.

5. *Add extra air pressure.* If you put added weight in your car, stop at the first gas station and put two or three pounds of extra pressure in your rear tires.

6. *If a snowplow blocks your driveway entrance.* If you have to "blast out" . . .

Never attempt it when other traffic is moving or pedestrians are near. Wait until the street is empty.

Never attempt it if there is a tree, a pole, or a parked car near your driveway. Cars sometimes swerve sideways in the attempt and could hit a nearby object.

When you see a safe chance, aim your car straight at the snow pile, get it rolling at a steady but moderate speed, and let the car's weight and momentum carry you through the snow. Be sure you have enough speed (say, 10 mph) to carry you all the way through. Don't hit such a pile too slowly and then expect your engine to push you through. It won't. Your wheels will spin and you'll be stuck.

Expect your car to react violently but continue to steer straight.

Do not race your engine and spin your wheels if your car refuses

Snow: Spinning

Never spin wheels
even for an instant.
It just digs a "stuck" car in deeper

to go through. Stop immediately. With a little shoveling you may be able to back up for another try. If after stalling you spin your wheels, they will dig you in worse than before.

After you get through the pile, open the hood and check to see if snow has clogged your radiator, as mentioned earlier.

All this will get you out through a couple of feet of soft, fresh snow piled by a plow.

But . . .

Don't attempt it if the snow depth approaches three feet. And don't try it on any old, frozen snow pile—even a small one—because rock-hard snow can damage your car.

7. *If you get stuck: the right and wrong way to "rock" a car.* Some cars when stuck in deep snow can be quite neatly "rocked" out. But this should be attempted only with standard-transmission (stick-shift) cars. Rocking, unlike the slow "starting pad" procedure outlined below, is a rapid process. By careful footwork on gas and clutch you get your car to roll forward barely an inch or two. Instantly—as soon as it moves—release clutch and let it roll back. It will do this—it will "bounce back" slightly—because in trying to move forward out of its rut, it has actually formed and climbed part way up a little hill—a mound of packed snow or ice in front of each tire.

When the car rolls backward down that little hill—merely an inch or two—engage the clutch and once more roll it forward. This time the car will try to go farther. Let it move ahead three or four inches—no more. Disengage clutch and once more let it roll back. Keep repeating until you feel the car traveling a little farther on each rock. Then when you feel it ready to roll free, feed gas gently and move ahead.

Do not persist in rocking an automatic-transmission car! This can burn and ruin the many small brake and clutch discs that are contained in an expensive automatic transmission. Don't try to force an automatic-transmission car to rock out even though your owner's manual may say that this can be done.

8. *How to free an automatic-transmission car.* If it doesn't roll out on the first easy attempt—i.e., one easy rock forward and one backward—there are three things to do: (*a*) try the "starting pad" technique described below. That may work. If not, then (*b*) shovel out and apply grit (or rock salt) under tires or (*c*) use chains.

9. *Where and how to shovel.* One mistake drivers make is trying to use short-handled, wide-bladed householder-type snow shovels. These cause backbreaking work and are all but useless—because they won't

reach under the car where the real trouble is. Shoveling snow away from the wheels is useless if there is still tough snow jammed under axles, engine, and transmission!

To get at this hidden snow you need a light, narrow, long-handled scoop-type shovel or spade. Some snow-country drivers also keep a long-handled garden hoe in the car. An iron rake is excellent.

First, remove snow in front of and behind each wheel. But don't, as many drivers do, allow the shovel to dig under the tire tread. This simply drops the tire deeper into the snow, with the result that it is going to have to climb more of a "hill" in order to get out. And this is sometimes impossible.

Next, clear the axles and remove snow packed under gas tank and around tail pipe. (Here's where a hoe or rake helps.) Remove snow that is packed hard under the transmission (the large metal "bulge" that hangs underneath the driver's compartment). Also remove snow packed under the engine.

After digging around the wheels, leave your tires resting undisturbed on small mounds, an inch or two higher than all surrounding snow where you have shoveled. Now each wheel is elevated on its own little monument of compressed snow and ice. When you gently feed gas, the car will roll off the mound—and at last you have movement started. With quick but delicate footwork on the gas you can capture this first small impulse, increase it, and keep the car going.

In case the car does not go ahead on this first try, do not force it even for one split second or you'll dig in and have it all to do over again. Get out, quickly clear away any remaining trouble (you have already done most of the work), then try a second time. This time you can hardly fail.

10. *Straighten your wheels!* What causes many cars to stay stuck is simply drivers' failure to straighten front wheels. This is the first step highway maintenance crews take when they find a motorist stuck. It is surprising how often the crews find the car easy to move after that one correction.

So when you are bogged down, get out and see which way your wheels are turned. If possible, have someone watch and tell you when you have turned them absolutely straight ahead.

11. *Keep going!* Use your car's momentum. Let us suppose that you find yourself on an unplowed street or road. This is certainly no place to be driving if you can avoid it; but suppose you have a good and urgent reason. You find driving difficult. The snow is up to your hub-caps.

What you must remember now is that this snow is going to try to pack hard against the undersides of your car and stop you. And if you stop, you may not get going again.

So the trick now is to keep going (so long as it is safe). Make the car's forward momentum work. The biggest error in deep snow is stopping at the wrong time. At the bottom of small hills, for example, some drivers get timid, stop to look the hill over—and can't get started again.

Is it dangerous to keep going? Yes, sometimes, of course it is, especially if other cars are near. But at other times it is dangerous *not* to keep going, because you may stall in the face of oncoming cars and be hit. Only you can be the judge, since no two conditions are ever exactly alike. The important thing, as in all driving, is to use good judgment.

12. *Never spin your wheels* if the rear of your car tries to swerve around or if the car stops moving. Once you stall and let your wheels spin, you are in trouble. The good snow driver never lets spinning get a start. He has two good reasons: (1) Spinning tires get hot and melt the snow. Then cold from the ground creeps in and turns the water to slick ice. (2) Spinning wheels dig deep holes and lock themselves in.

What to do if your wheels start to spin. Stop them instantly! Get out and see what is happening. After loosening snow with a shovel, throwing sand or grit under the tires helps. There are also commercial sprays sold in auto-supply shops which are said to give a tire better traction on ice.

But—before you try to drive on, wait and let your tires cool. Warm tires tend to do more spinning. Cool tires have a greater ability to dig out.

13. *Don't turn the wheels!* Next to lack of tractive weight and wheel spinning, the other big cause of stalls is—turning.

Remember that your front wheels obligingly cut a track for your rear wheels—the real workers. Nothing, however, cuts a track for those front wheels. They must fight constantly against a barrier of snow.

Just as long as you can keep them perfectly straight they will usually knife into that snow wall quite easily. But when you turn them they present a wider area of resistance. This throws a blocking force against the front wheels, overloads the rear driving wheels, causes loss of traction, and can spin you into immobility. So, to keep going in deep snow, never turn your front wheels when you can avoid it.

14. *If you must use chains.* Some drivers have trouble putting on chains. It's really quite simple and can be done in a few moments if you have good-quality, easy-to-fasten reinforced chains and use this method:

Hang chain loosely over tire from top. (If there's room above the tire, between it and the fender, you may not even have to use a jack.)

Reach behind tire and clamp the two dangling chain ends together where they meet at the ground. Make them as taut as you can. On many cars it's easy. No great strain is needed. But you may have to lie on your back in snow.

Now clamp the chain ends together on the outside of the tire, also where they meet near the ground. You won't be able to get the chain very tight at first.

Next, run the car forward six or eight feet. This will "set" the chain on the tire with the proper tightness.

Now unfasten the outside clamp, tighten the chain a bit, then refasten the clamp to another link.

Don't change the inside clamp—the one you fastened on the opposite side of the tire. Only the outside clamp needs adjustment.

15. *Use a "starting pad."* If your car is parked in the open, you can try a trick that lumberjacks use when deep snow falls far back in the Maine woods.

With all possible weight in the rear of your car, gingerly back up two inches only.

Now roll forward six inches.

And next, before the tires can sink in, roll back again. But this time go just a few inches farther.

Then immediately go forward gently a second time. (Do not try to "rock" the car violently forward and backward by putting the engine first in drive and then in reverse.)

If you do this with great care, you will soon roll out a hard-packed "pad," or starting runway, upon which you can get needed starting momentum.

WHEN THE ROAD TURNS TO ICE

Most ordinary tires have little traction on ice. Don't rely on them. They may fool you. You may get along all right for a short distance at slow speed. But if you then find it necessary to apply brakes, speed up, or climb a hill, your car may spin around so fast it will leave you breathless.

What should you do if a road suddenly turns icy and you lack chains or special tires? Pull off and wait (*a*) until a highway sander comes along or (*b*) several big trucks with tire chains have used the road. Huge truck chains chop up ice and sometimes help keep other traffic going. (But beware of hills!)

Excellent on ice are studded tires—four of them. Studded tires on all four wheels give amazing control under some glare-ice conditions. So do tire chains. But chains make for "lumpy" riding.

Studded tires used on the rear wheels only help a great deal, but there is still danger that your front wheels may skid off the road on turns. Studded tires, of course, are tires into which dozens of small plastic or steel studs are embedded. These look like small bullets and bite into the ice.

Snow tires are slightly better than ordinary tires on smooth ice—but only slightly better. Don't rely on them too much.

Note: If you use studs or chains, you may sometimes feel the rear of your car start to slide alarmingly sideways—toward the ditch or the next lane. If this happens, simply feed a little gas. The wheels will instantly "power out" of the slide, and your car will straighten out.

If you use studded tires, don't expect them to bite and slow you down instantly. They sometimes slide a few feet after you apply brakes—perhaps ten to twenty feet—and just as you think you are going into a long, dangerous skid they take hold and slow you. But expect that brief moment of sliding when you apply brakes at a corner or try to slow down behind a car that is stopping ahead of you.

SPECIAL WARNING ABOUT SLUSH

An innocent-looking road coated with two to four inches of wet, slushy snow may well be the most treacherous road you will ever have to face. The whole trouble is: It doesn't look slippery. But it is as slick as ice!

An icy road looks slippery, so you drive cautiously. A snowy road evokes caution because it looks dangerous. But since dirty gray slush looks deceptively safe, it traps many drivers.

Slush Skids

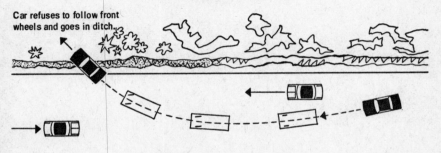

Car refuses to follow front wheels and goes in ditch.

Driving in slush you may feel quite secure in trying to overtake another car at 45 mph on an ordinary two-way road. And, indeed, you pull out of line gradually, accelerate carefully and safely, and get ahead of the other car. You are now in the left lane, and your accelerated speed is about 48 to 50 mph.

You turn your wheels slightly to the right, as usual, in order to pull back into your proper lane. Your car obediently heads back toward its lane, and then, of course, you turn the wheels to the left in order to straighten it out.

And this is where slush springs its trap. When you turn to the left, the car simply refuses to respond. With front wheels skidding uselessly it runs into the ditch. The sloping right side of the road, plus the slush, plus your rather brisk straightening of the wheels (now that you feel safely back on your side) have tricked you.

Three or four inches of wet slush on a super-road calls for extraordinary caution. Cars exceeding 50 mph simply cannot cope with it and often spin around or run off the road. Again the big trouble is: It looks so safe but isn't!

CHAPTER XXI

EMERGENCIES

STAB-AND-STEER TECHNIQUE

AN UNSKILLED DRIVER relies on his brakes alone to stop him in a sudden crisis. The expert, instead, relies on a technique that could be called "brake-and-steer" or, more graphically, "stab-and-steer."

Consider the drawing below: a panic situation. A huge boulder rolls off a dump truck. It stops in your lane, two hundred feet ahead. The road is dry. Your speed is 55 mph. According to widely used stopping-

Braking

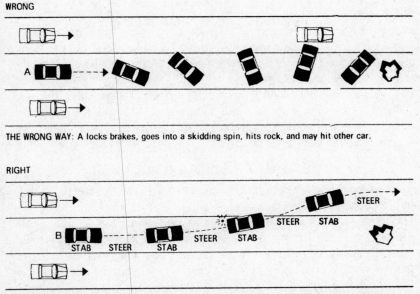

THE WRONG WAY: A locks brakes, goes into a skidding spin, hits rock, and may hit other car.

THE RIGHT WAY: B stab-steers around obstacle, and other cars are warned. He can even use turn signal to advantage.

distance tables it will take you at least 400 feet to stop your car after you see the boulder.

How will you handle this situation? You will have less than half the stopping distance that you need.

The inept driver will simply clamp his foot to the brake pedal in a "panic stop" attempt. This will immediately lock his wheels and throw him into a long, screaming skid. And since a car skidding with locked wheels cannot be steered, he will probably hit the boulder—or another car.

Other drivers, remembering that "brake pumping" helps to avoid skids on ice or very slippery roads, may give the brake pedal one or two pumps with their foot. But then, seeing that they cannot stop in time, they too will panic, lock the brakes, spin around, and slide directly against the obstacle.

The expert takes a different approach. He simply does not try to stop in a hopeless situation. Instead, he tries to (1) cut speed sharply and (2) steer around the obstruction.

In order to slow down while keeping steering control he *does* pump his brakes. But he doesn't pump in the halfhearted manner of some drivers. At high speed the brakes must be stabbed—hard—but just for a split second. This locks up the wheels, prevents steering, and starts a short skid. But just as the skid begins, he foils it by releasing his brakes—again for just a split second. That's all the time it takes to stop the skid. And in that split second he starts steering again.

Instantly the expert stabs and releases the brakes once more. With such fractional release he can steer. And if he makes four or five stabs in the two hundred feet ahead between him and disaster, he can usually steer around any obstruction.

This stab-and-steer technique has further merit: It alerts other drivers, gives them a chance to pull aside and make room. They see the car lurch, hear the tires, see it start veering slightly to left or right. And they have time to maneuver out of the way.

THE TRUTH ABOUT SKIDDING

It is commonly believed that you can control a skid by steering in the same direction that your rear wheels skid.

This is good in theory. And it works wonders around town in little slow-speed skids on ice or wet leaves if you don't keep your brakes on! In fact, it's really what most drivers do anyhow. They naturally try to steer their skidding cars back into the proper lane. But the rule confuses some drivers, especially beginners. In the panic of a skid they don't steer soon enough—because they start to wonder, "Which way *are* my rear wheels going?" And so the rule might be simpler if revised to read merely, "In a skid steer your car the way you want it to go."

But while it works in some situations, there are a few things wrong with this idea.

In a bad skid it works only during the first second or two. Once your car veers around more than a few degrees, you can't steer the way you want to go, because your wheels won't turn that much!

And if your wheels are locked by your brakes, as in most bad skids, it doesn't make any difference which way you try to turn. You can't steer anyhow. (In fact, if the skid becomes a spin, you can't even turn the wheel fast enough to keep up with the changing direction of your car.)

In a high-speed, dry-road skid, if by releasing the brakes you can steer at all, it may be better to steer moderately. On a flat, wide surface it sometimes pays to let the car go the way it wants to go if you are lucky and there is no danger of hitting something. Steer by the feel of the car. The average car takes pretty good care of itself in a skid unless it hits something, or "trips" over a low curb or bump. It may even spin around (perhaps several times) on a flat, smooth surface without turning over.

During a skid don't feed gas in an attempt to power the car back into its lane. This can instantly turn even a mild skid into a wild spin.

The essential facts to remember are these:

1. It is impossible to control any skid if your brakes are locked.
2. The only safe rule for controlling skids is never get into one. They are terribly dangerous.
3. If a skid does start, act fast—in the first second or two. Steer the way you want the car to go—but don't overdo it. Take your foot off the brake. Your best protection in a skid—your one hope of coming out of it—is four free-rolling wheels. A free-rolling wheel has enormous ability to straighten your car out without your help—if you will just give it a chance. It bites hard into the road. But it cannot do this if you (1) apply brakes or (2) use the accelerator.

If a skid spins your car around so far that steering is impossible, don't twist the wheel. Hold it firmly. Cars go through some unexpected lurching and bucking in a spin. This is quite violent and can unseat you unless your seat belt is fastened and you have a good grip on the wheel.

The Slippery-Road Skid. The same principles apply with one exception. Skids on ice, mud, wet leaves (and sometimes merely slick rainy surfaces) often take place without any braking at all. With no warning the rear of the car simply begins a sideways slide-out. Or on a curve or change of lanes the front wheels may stubbornly refuse to steer and may go into a slide without turning the car as they should.

When the rear of the car starts to slide, do not use the brakes. And do not accelerate. It does sometimes pay to "feather" the gas slightly, feeding just enough to keep the rear wheels from slowing down suddenly and acting as a brake. When they do this, they can make the skid worse.

Once your car is straightened out, try to steer perfectly straight—if on a very slick surface—and decelerate very gradually until you have it under full control.

The Downhill Skid on a Slippery Road. If, while descending an icy hill, your car begins to slide out of control you have three choices:

1. Run off on the right edge, which is usually gritty, and try for better traction. Avoid using brakes unless absolutely necessary.

2. If the hill is steep and dangerous (especially if other cars are coming up or down) and all hope of control seems gone, it is sometimes best to look for a soft spot in a snow-filled ditch or in a snow pile and lay the car into it as gently as possible—now—before speed increases and you become a dangerous runaway.

3. If the hill looks safe below and nothing else will work, it is sometimes possible to let the car run and hope that your four free-rolling wheels will straighten you out. They may. Then steer perfectly straight until you are down the hill or on a safe surface again.

4. Downshifting *before* you start down a slippery hill sometimes gives smoother control than can be achieved with brakes, but it can also cause a spin unless very cautiously employed.

The Uphill Skid on a Slippery Road. This usually happens when someone feeds gas while trying to climb a snow-covered hill or one coated with ice or slush. The car goes part way up. But then, as gas is fed, it suddenly swerves around and across the road.

This is an extremely dangerous skid, not so much because of what can happen during the skid as what can happen afterward. Your car now may be stalled in snow, unable to move. It is a sitting duck waiting to be hit by others that may skid on the hill.

But an uphill skid can easily be avoided by a driver who has developed a sense of "car feel." Don't slow your car too much before starting to climb the hill. (Many drivers slow down more timidly than necessary before starting up. Care is needed, but excess timidity can be dangerous.)

Climbing a Slippery Hill

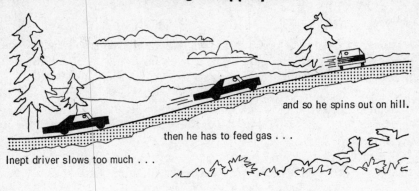

and so he spins out on hill.

then he has to feed gas . . .

Inept driver slows too much . . .

THE WRONG WAY

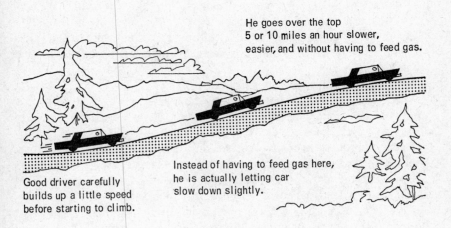

He goes over the top
5 or 10 miles an hour slower,
easier, and without having to feed gas.

Instead of having to feed gas here,
he is actually letting car
slow down slightly.

Good driver carefully
builds up a little speed
before starting to climb.

THE RIGHT WAY

An expert will start up a slippery hill as fast as conditions and common sense permit. But he does not accelerate on the hill! Instead, he feeds gas and increases speed to maximum safe limits before he starts to climb. Thus he builds up in advance a bit of extra speed that he can "throw away" as he climbs. Instead of having to feed gas, which is dangerous, he is actually able to let his car slow down slightly as he approaches the top. If, for example, it is possible to take the bottom of the hill at a safe 45 mph, he may gradually decelerate until he is going over the top at 40 or even 35. By so doing he really has safe "free rolling wheels" all the way up. He really let his car's momentum carry him up; no skid-inducing extra thrust by the rear wheels is necessary at any time.

"CADENCE BRAKING" FOR A QUICK, STRAIGHT STOP

There is one kind of braking that will stop a conventional front-engine car in a panic emergency in a straight line and in a very short distance. It also works well with some rear-engine cars.

A. R. Slotemaker, the European skid expert and consultant to the Renault Company, calls it "cadence braking." He teaches it to advanced drivers in England (where, it is interesting to note, advanced drivers get special certificates).

Cadence braking is really an advanced form of brake pumping or stab braking. You hit the brake very suddenly and very hard to lock your wheels for just an instant—in a very brief skid.

But it differs from pumping or stabbing in one important respect: Instead of hitting the brake pedal in a random series of fast stabs, you hit it in time with the car's own natural rocking rhythm (or cadence).

The diagram shows how it works.

Even while going downhill the author by using this method has brought a heavy car to a full stop from 55 mph in approximately five seconds.

Why does cadence braking work?

When you stab the brakes hard, any car tends to rock forward on its springs. Professionals call this a "nosedive." Then the car instantly recovers and rocks back.

Cadence braking keeps the car rocking and nosediving until it stops. You use the car's natural rocking rhythm to help you. By locking brakes briefly when the car is in a nosedive, you cause it to throw more weight on the front wheels, where weight does the most good.

This helps because in any conventional car front wheels are your best stoppers. In fact, on many cars the front brakes are actually bigger and stronger.

Cadence Braking

Car will leave a series of short, straight tire burns (skid marks).

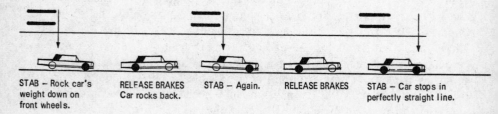

STAB – Rock car's weight down on front wheels.   RELFASE BRAKES Car rocks back.   STAB – Again.   RELEASE BRAKES   STAB – Car stops in perfectly straight line.

When a perfect straight-line stop is called for, cadence braking can help. If there are obstructions to be steered around, an expert feels his way with the stab-and-steer method previously described.

Note: Before you ever use cadence braking, it pays to practice (in a safe place) so that you will know your own car's rocking rhythm. No two cars have the same cadence.

THE STALLED-CAR EMERGENCY

Running out of gasoline has always been an inconvenience, but in recent years it has also become a serious risk. A car suddenly out of gas on a fast modern road is in great danger of being hit. In fact, the safety patrols on one busy superhighway now estimate that if you can't reach a shoulder and have to stop in a traveled lane, your car will probably be hit within twenty minutes. This is an average based on the experience of motorists who have stopped in traveled lanes on that particular highway.

It is wise never to venture onto superhighway traffic if there is the slightest indication—in advance—that anything at all could be wrong with your car. Any unusual sound, any thumping tire or sputtering engine, or any sign of overheating should be investigated and corrective action taken before you commit yourself to traffic.

Be careful, too, to check your gasoline level. If you think you have just about enough gas to reach your destination, don't try it. A headwind may spring up, push against your car, and cause your tank to run dry sooner than you anticipated. Also remember that some gasoline gauges are deceptive. They may indicate that a tank is one-eighth to one-quarter full when, in fact, it is nearly empty. Never let a deceptive gas gauge lure you into a fuel emergency.

And no wise driver should be fooled by the common saying that "when a gauge reads empty, you still have two or three gallons left." This used to be true, but in the case of many cars when the gauge says empty it is empty. There is no extra gasoline left.

Often you will have a few minutes' advance warning before your tank runs dry. If you ever smell gas, check the gauge. The odor sometimes comes just before the gas runs out. Another warning may be a brief misfire in the engine, after which it recovers and runs steadily. A third warning is a gasoline-gauge needle that suddenly swings from "quarter full" to "empty" when you turn a corner or a sharp curve. In any of these situations the time to get off the road—and out of the way of traffic—is at that moment.

If your engine stops, it is vital to coast immediately to a shoulder—while the car still has momentum. Condition yourself in advance to think of this; otherwise, when the emergency does come, you will be so surprised that you will waste precious time. You may in error devote your efforts to getting the engine started again when you should be pulling off the road before the car stops rolling.

The Reserve Tank. Some drivers carry a spare tank of gas in the trunk. This has prevented many an emergency. But it is also risky because in a collision the spare container could burst and fill the car with flammable liquid or explosive fumes. If you do take such a risk, use a strong steel container (such as a Jeep "jerry can"). Some plastic containers break open easily, especially when cold and brittle.

It is worth remembering that your car may stall in a traveled lane from which you cannot reach the shoulder, because access is cut off by moving cars and trucks. Thus if your gasoline ever should run low and you think it is ready to run out, do all your driving in the lane nearest the shoulder—until you reach a gas station or a safe turnout where you can seek help.

If you do stall in a traveled lane and can't reach a shoulder, you will find it necessary to act very quickly as follows:

Turn your hazard flashers on.

Light your other rear lights. Flash them once or twice—if there is time to do so safely. Turn on your car's inside (dome) light.

Get everyone—including yourself—out of the car and safely away from it.

Leave a door open (if there is room without endangering other cars). This helps get attention long before other cars approach.

Realize that the car may be hit. Decide in which direction it may be thrown or which way a striking car might skid after the collision. Remember that bumpers, fenders, and glass fly some distance. *Place your passengers safely out of this risk area.*

Quickly light red fire flares and protect the rear of your car. (See "How to Use Flame Flares," page 157.)

If there is time in daytime, have someone raise the engine hood and leave it up. The reason: A raised hood rising above a car can be seen far back above traffic. At night a raised hood may do no good.

Lower the radio antenna. Tie a large white cloth to it (or even someone's shirt, if the weather is warm), then raise it full height. A white handkerchief may help but is less easily seen. Don't underestimate the importance of this warning flag, for you are actually dealing now in a very real life-or-death crisis for somebody.

Quickly send someone far back down the road to wave a coat, a red sweater, or at night a large white cloth.

Do not permit anyone—especially a woman or child—to try to flag down traffic by standing in the lane in which your car has stopped. And be sure to warn your flagman to stand on the shoulder and to watch out for cars that will skid off the road when drivers suddenly discover your stalled car.

Be sure that whoever waves a cloth waves it high. Otherwise it cannot be seen above cars. And be sure to send him far back. It is sheer suicide for you or anyone else to stand close behind your car trying to wave down fast traffic. The warning should be given at least one-tenth of a mile (roughly a long city block) back and preferably farther. This distance is needed in order to give drivers time to change lanes in a hurry without colliding with each other.

If anyone slows down, ask him to notify police or a garage quickly. Do not encourage anyone to stop behind your car, for he may get hit. Helpful drivers, the good Samaritans of the highway, often forget this in their desire to be of assistance. Anyone who stops to help should pull his car safely off the road.

Don't put your trust in a small waving flashlight at night. Drivers approaching at speeds over 40 or 45 mph often cannot see it at all. Its flickering beam may look like just another roadside reflector or beer can.

If you keep a flashlight in your car (as all drivers should), keep a big one—the most powerful one you can get. Flash it intermittently, *directly* at oncoming cars. Don't wave it from side to side or it won't be seen. Even a big flashlight is not always noticed.

Don't put much trust in small gimmicky "warning lights" or small red reflectors. Even some of the devices professional truck drivers use are virtually invisible until the last few seconds. Others are hopelessly dim or get blown over by traffic. If you buy such a warning device, be sure to buy a big and powerful one.

IF YOUR RADIATOR BOILS OVER

In town a boiling engine may not be too great a problem because it is quickly noticed and mechanical help is usually near.

But on the road your first notice may be the hot smell of metal, which means that your engine is suffering—indeed, may already be damaged. Another warning (in some cars) is an odd buzzing sound from the engine. Or a passing motorist seeing the steam of your boiling engine may signal you frantically by hand or with his lights.

For any such situation, of course, most cars have a red "overheat" warning light that is supposed to flash on your dashboard. Such lights don't always work, however.

Whatever the circumstances, stop at once in a safe place. There are now two important "don'ts."

Don't try to drive to the next gas station. (This ruins many engines that could be saved.) And don't let just anyone remove the radiator cap to let steam out and to pour water in. Radiators contain explosive pressure—even after the steam dies down. Amateurs who lift the caps too soon or without knowing how have been badly scalded. A mechanic knows how to loosen the cap first, by giving it a slight turn to the "safety notch," and then letting the hot water gush downward without exploding in his face. After this, he removes the cap.

If no mechanic is around but a friendly motorist stops to help, it is quite possible he may find that your only trouble is a small leak that has let all the water run out. Fifteen minutes (no sooner) after the steaming stops, he may be able to remove the cap cautiously and add enough water to get you to a garage. (Run your engine slowly while he adds the water.)

Otherwise your best bet is to send for a mechanic. You may have a broken radiator hose, a loose fan belt, a faulty thermostat, a frozen radiator, or other problems. All of the foregoing are easily fixed in most service stations.

HOW TO STOP A RUNAWAY CAR

One of the most critical emergencies is the runaway car. Is there anything you can do about it? Here are some reasons for this occurrence and suggestions for handling the situation.

A car can run away with you inside for three reasons: (1) The brakes may fail, (2) the accelerator pedal may stick down, or (3) brakes and engine resistance (compression) may simply be insufficient to hold it on a steep mountain grade.

When Brakes Fail. In a car with a dual braking system, chances are that only two wheel brakes will fail at once. This system is designed so that two brakes continue to work if the other two fail. Older cars do not have this safety device.

If your two rear-wheel brakes fail, you are not necessarily in trouble at all. Your front brakes are still holding; and they are your best brakes anyhow because they are generally bigger, have more holding power, and (contrary to the belief of some drivers) will stop you in a perfectly straight line without any help from the rear brakes. Your car will *not* try to spin around. You may not even be aware that your rear brakes have failed, except that you will notice that your car does not stop quite so fast.

But if your two front-wheel brakes fail, you may be in quite a lot of trouble if a sudden stop on a wet road becomes necessary. That's because a hard application of the only remaining (rear) brakes may lock your rear wheels. And it is this (and not a front-wheel lock) that can spin your car out of control.

Some cars have "crisscross" (diagonal) braking systems. The right front wheel and the left rear wheel operate on one hydraulic system, while the left front and right rear wheels use the second system. Thus when one system fails, you still have one front and one rear brake working and the danger of a spin-out is less than when the two front brakes fail.

If all brakes fail in traffic and you suddenly find yourself in a runaway car, then there are several things you can do. All involve calculated danger but may help nonetheless.

1. Quickly try to "pump up pressure" in the brake system by pumping the brake pedal rapidly. This sometimes works.

2. Apply emergency (parking) brake carefully, making sure you do not cause a skid. Some emergency brakes will stop a car gradually; others are quite useless because they haven't been kept in adjustment.

3. Shift down to low gear and then quickly kill the engine. (Don't kill the engine unless you have a standard-shift model.) Shifting down abruptly at high speed can slow a standard-shift car sharply, but on a slippery surface it can cause a spin. Care should be used. You are now using your engine as a brake (compression braking). After speed is reduced, begin applying the emergency brake.

In some automatic-transmission cars a fairly strong engine-braking effect is felt when you downshift; in others the engine has relatively little effect. (Be sure always to test your car in a safe place and *know* how much engine braking you can count on.)

To downshift a standard-transmission car, of course, you (*a*) declutch, (*b*) rev up the engine a bit, (*c*) shift down to the next position, then (*d*) remove foot from clutch pedal.

To downshift an automatic-transmission car, you simply move the lever from normal drive position to a lower position.

Note to power-steering users: You don't have to be afraid that cutting off the ignition will put your power steering out of use so long as you do not shift the engine to neutral. By leaving the transmission engaged you make sure that the car itself will keep the engine turning. And therefore the power-steering unit will continue to work. Only in the final seconds just before your car stops may the power steering be less effective. It may cease working and you may have to wrestle the car manually for the last few feet to a safe stop.

Rubbing Off Speed. If all else fails, it is sometimes possible to "rub off speed" by carefully steering a car against (a) a guard rail, (b) a row of small wooden posts, or (c) a row of small (never large) trees or dense bushes. Obviously this presents great dangers and is worth trying only in extreme emergency.

It is also possible sometimes to steer a runaway car up a grassy slope or into a thick snowbank or out into a level field. But make sure there are no rocks or other hard objects—and, of course, you have to determine this at a glance!

Never under any circumstances steer against a large tree or utility pole. And never come in contact with a concrete culvert, abutment, or foundation of any type (not even the small concrete foundation of an ordinary highway sign; all these are real killers).

Steering to a Safe Stop. The most satisfactory solution to a runaway-car emergency, of course, is simply to steer down the road, miss other traffic (with luck), and wait for your car to stop safely (on the shoulder). The author once felt his brakes fail on a superhighway. By luck he was able to coast up an exit ramp and he let the up-slope stop his car.

If on a fast superhighway you cannot reach a safe shoulder or police help, it may be best not to stop but to continue under control in low gear at a suitable speed until you reach a safe turnoff.

When Accelerator Pedals Stick. This happens now and then, especially to older cars. If the pedal jams down against the floor your engine may race and you may be shocked and startled. If there is time, try to pry it up with your foot; this sometimes works. If not and your speed is high, shift engine to lower gearing, cut off ignition, apply brakes and coast to a safe (shoulder) stop. Have pedal fixed at once. Otherwise it will stick again.

Note: If you ever have to switch your engine off in order to slow your car, *don't* remove the key from the ignition lock or you may lock the steering!

ACCIDENTS

WHAT TO DO IF YOU SEE ONE

WHEN YOU SEE AN ACCIDENT that has just happened, what should you do?

If competent-looking helpers are already at the scene, you might stop in a safe place and inquire whether your help is needed. If not, get in your car and drive on. Too many people at an accident scene lead to confusion—and additional accidents.

But suppose you are among the first to arrive and you see someone in trouble. A motorist may be trapped in a car. He may be hurt.

What are your moral obligations? Morally any decent motorist would consider himself bound to stop (in a safe place) and offer assistance within the limits of his skills, experience, and strength. Anyone well trained might, of course, be qualified to offer first aid. A strong man might help lift an overturned car to free a victim. Someone who knows cars might help to disconnect a battery cable to prevent risk of fire.

What are your legal responsibilities? Do you have to stop at an accident scene and offer help? Legally you do not. You may keep right on going. But if you don't stop, remember this: Some day other motorists may go on past and "look the other way" when you need help.

IF YOU ARE THE FIRST AT AN ACCIDENT SCENE *

You're driving home from a trip when the fellow ahead hits a curve too fast. He skids, panics, locks brakes. There's a scream of tires. His car smacks a culvert with a sickening sound, then flips over.

---

* This article, first published in *Popular Science* and reprinted in *Reader's Digest*, won commendation from the American Red Cross.

Dead silence.

You're what the police call the "first on the scene." What do you do now?

Your first instinct is to run to the car and start hauling people out. Don't. Highway rescue experts estimate that eighty percent of the people hurt in cars are pulled out by frantic rescuers—and many are made worse or even killed.

Every crash is different so there are no rules. But here are tips to guide you:

What to do first. Park your car far enough away from the crash scene to protect it. Turn off the key of the wrecked car to prevent fire. Then take a few moments to think. What are the conditions at the scene? What else can happen? How can police be notified quickly?

Help protect the scene. Two cars collided recently on a heavily traveled turnpike. Three people were slightly hurt. But moments later five were dead. Reason: Rescuers ran first to help the injured instead of running to flag down approaching high-speed traffic.

Thus it is often far more important to "protect the scene" than to go at once to the injured. Flag down the first cars, have the drivers pull off the road, and ask them to go back to warn and slow traffic. If it's a two-lane road, send your flagmen both ways—and not fifty or a hundred feet, but five hundred or even a thousand, where they'll do some good.

Dealing with the victims. If the victims of the crash are still in the car, do everything you can to guard against danger of fire. By talking to them, determine who is hurt and assist out of the wreck anyone who is not hurt. But if any complain of pain or are bleeding severely or are unconscious or in shock, experienced rescuers advise you to leave them where they are until (1) an ambulance comes or (2) you can find trained first-aid workers to move them.

Two doctors told us: "We often see people die whom we could have saved if they had not been moved by volunteers who had no first-aid training. Even a victim with a broken backbone can usually be saved if allowed to lie unmoved. But well-meaning people often lift them out of wrecks, stuff them into the back seats of cars, and rush them to us. In doing this, they twist the spine, and the broken sections are hopelessly displaced. Jagged bones also penetrate the body.

"It is bad enough to lift or roll a badly injured person if you know how. It is dangerous in the extreme to let untrained rescuers carry them and let their bodies jackknife."

Send two drivers to notify police. Hail at least two passing cars and send them in opposite directions to find telephones and call police. Many motorists make the mistake of sending only one car, and sometimes no one at all is sent. Police say it is wise to send as many as four or five cars in each direction.

"If only one car is sent, its driver may go ten miles, find no phone, and then give up," police say.

What to do about lifting cars. "Thousands of people get hurt all over again because motorists try to lift cars, find they can't, and have to let the cars fall back," said one police veteran. "Don't make the mistake of trying to lift a car bodily until you have eight or ten strong men. There are times when four men can lift one side of a light car—but if you try this, be sure you aren't pushing the other side down on someone."

If people are pinned in the wreck. Often accident victims appear to be trapped when they are merely held by a foot twisted under a seat, rescue squads say. Crawl in and release the foot. If they are unhurt, they can get out.

The squads often find people trapped on the floor under the dashboard. They can't get out because they can't lower their heads enough to clear the lower edge of the dash. "If they aren't injured, we merely push their heads down gently until they can pull clear," the squads say.

Now and then it is necessary to straighten out the car body before someone can be freed. It is far better to bend the wreckage than to cut it. Some excited rescuers bring acetylene torches. "We fight this tooth and nail because of fire danger," one squad reported. "We get a tow truck to hook its chain to the wreckage and bend it an inch at a time."

If you find a driver trapped between his seat and the steering wheel, pressure on him often can be eased by the mere expedient of releasing the catch and sliding the seat back.

Are people lying in the road? If you leave them there, they may be run over. But moving may aggravate their injuries.

Which should you do?

Police say it is better to leave seriously injured people where they are but take extraordinary steps to guard them. Police often place their cars squarely across the road, with 360-degree flashers going to warn traffic. If in dire emergency you decide to do this, place your car at least fifty feet away because if it gets hit by traffic, it may be pushed against the victims. Also, police say, turn your car to face traffic and blink your headlights rapidly at approaching vehicles. Have all cars stopped at the scene turn on their four-way hazard flashers or turn signals to get attention of fast-approaching cars.

But what about fire? A frantic fear of fire often causes volunteers to haul out accident victims who should not have been moved. But how can you know what to do?

Rescuers say you can relax a bit if fire hasn't started in the car when you get there. About one car in seven catches fire in a crash. But if fire does not start immediately, it rarely starts afterward.

Fire in wiring usually begins smoldering under the hood or dashboard. Your decision on what to do should be based on whether there is gasoline leaking that could suddenly cause a burst of fire. Rescue teams usually do these things: (1) Disconnect the battery (being careful not to let the hot wire hit metal parts and cause sparks), (2) locate the fire, (3) attack it with fire extinguishers, dirt, or blanket. (If you have no extinguisher, borrow one from a passing truck.)

While waiting for an ambulance. If you are skilled at first aid, you may find you can render some assistance. If not, do these things:

1. Hail passing cars until you do find trained first-aiders, a doctor, or a nurse. In some states doctors can be spotted by MD plates, nurses by RN insignia.

2. Put blankets over the injured to keep them warm (but not too warm).

3. Loosen collars, ties, and belts to help breathing.

4. Do what you can to slow heavy bleeding (see page 160).

5. Send someone to find boards (or even to borrow a door from a house) on which trained first-aiders may carry victims flat if an ambulance fails to arrive.

6. Locate a truck on which victims can be carried flat if quick transportation is needed.

7. Talk to the injured; encourage them. Never tell them anyone else has been killed or is badly hurt.

"We even hold their hands," a rescue man told me. "This is very important. A firm handgrip seems to give them courage. Tell them help is coming and that they'll be fine."

IF YOU HAVE AN ACCIDENT

If you should ever have a collision with another car (or cars), you are going to make a very surprising discovery: After it is over you may have a great deal of trouble remembering what actually happened. Where did the other car (cars) come from? Who signaled first? Which car did you see first? You may forget all this in the excitement.

If you have already had an accident, you know how easily this can happen. And you may also have learned that no two people ever see things alike.

If cars collide in a legally reportable accident:

1. If you're not hurt, get out and (as noted on page 152) take quick action to protect the scene. Other cars, coming fast, often collide with those involved in accidents.

2. Attend to any injured and send for police. Police will call medical help if you tell them it is needed.

3. Be sure ignition keys are off and that no one is smoking even though you do not smell gas. (Gas may start to drip shortly.)

4. Attend to any injured. Write down (don't try to remember) license numbers of other vehicles involved, lest any hit-run driver decides to leave the scene in violation of law.

5. Exchange license and registration data with other drivers.

6. Make no impulsive admission (as drivers often do) such as, "It was all my fault." This may create legal problems later. And in addition, subsequent investigation often proves that the driver who thinks he was at fault may not have been to blame or wholly to blame at all.

7. Note carefully the extent of injuries (or lack of them) among all other persons involved. Note down their comments. Write all this down, because it is easily forgotten.

8. Get names and addresses of witnesses. Write down their license numbers.

9. If you have a camera, get photographs immediately. These should show (*a*) the general overall scene, (*b*) position of your car and the other car(s), (*c*) length and direction of skid marks leading to each car (very important later in reconstructing a true story of what happened). In addition, show the condition of tires on each car, especially any badly worn or bald ones. Photograph pertinent signs, lights, curves.

10. If you have no camera, borrow or rent one, or send home for one, if you live nearby.

11. Whether you do or do not use a camera, draw a complete diagram of the scene on paper. Show the road, curves, traffic lights, driveways, crossroads, buildings. Mark down the position of each car and where it came from. Show where the center line was.

12. When police arrive, cooperate fully and ask police also to seek witnesses' names.

13. When a tow truck arrives, remember this: on most roads you can choose your own tow service or garage. You do not have to accept the one suggested or called by police. (In some areas a few police have a "working arrangement" with certain favored tow-truck operators. It is true that on a few super-roads and parkways, certain tow trucks are licensed to operate exclusively and you must employ them— but only as far as the nearest exit. There you can have any garage of your choice take over.

Never let any tow-truck operator take your car away until you know what the cost will be. (Some have been known to charge as much as twenty-five dollars for towing a car a few feet to an exit.) Rates are usually required to be posted on the side of the truck itself.

Never let any tow truck leave with your car until you have noted down the name of the garage and its address—also required to be written on the truck. Some drivers have trouble locating their own cars after they have been towed away.

14. If your car has an automatic transmission, do not permit a tow-truck operator to tow it by the front end if he has more than a few blocks to go or if he will have to drive (as on some roads where minimum speed limits prevail) more than 35 mph. Forward-towing for long distances or at high speed can ruin an automatic transmission. He should either tow your car backward (on the front wheels) or else he should disconnect the drive shaft under the car. Never ride in a towed car.

15. Notify your insurance company as quickly as possible—the sooner the better. This protects you. The adjuster should see your car within hours or even at the accident scene.

16. Get repair estimates from three garages. But first find out their reputation. The cheapest garage sometimes gives you an excellent repair job—but not always.

SHOULD YOU GIVE YOUR NAME AS A WITNESS?

Suppose that you are standing on a sidewalk near an intersection. You see a collision between cars *A* and *B*. You note clearly that driver *A* was observing the law and that it was driver *B* who by violating a red traffic light caused the accident.

After the crash driver *A* asks you if you will tell him your name and address. You say, "Why?" He replies, "I may need witnesses to prove that I didn't cause the accident."

This happens to almost everyone at some time. Yet some drivers refuse to give their names and addresses, because they don't want to "get involved." In this refusal they are dead wrong—for two reasons.

In the first place, such drivers themselves are almost sure to need witnesses at some future date—possibly on several occasions. And by refusing to help driver *A* they are helping to tear down the concept of good citizenship and neighborliness that might help them, too, some day.

In the second place, they err in being afraid to get involved. It is true that some witnesses do get called to court. But most automobile cases today are being settled out of court. A witness may merely be asked by an attorney to state in a document what he saw. He may not even have to leave home. He may not even have to sign a statement. When driver *A* is in the right, merely the knowledge of others that he has good witnesses available if needed often protects him from unfair lawsuit or prosecution.

HOW TO USE FLAME FLARES

Next to the brilliant flashing cartop lights that police use, the best protection your car can have when stalled on or close to a fast-traveled lane is the sputtering red flame flare. Some experienced long-distance drivers, knowing this, carry as many as a dozen. Even for around-town driving you need at least three. They can be purchased inexpensively in many gas stations or auto-supply shops. Some burn for fifteen minutes, others for thirty minutes. In general thirty-minute flares are best.

The flashing red hazard lights with which all modern cars are equipped are also excellent protection but cannot be relied on in an emergency situation for a very simple reason: They are too close to the road to be seen except when a road is relatively free of traffic. On a busy road they are hidden by moving cars and trucks.

Furthermore, no warning light or reflector at or near your car is of much use on a crowded fast highway if it is hidden around a curve, behind a bridge abutment, or is otherwise obscured until the last moment of danger. To be of any real value on a fast highway it must be clearly seen by every other driver at least one-tenth of a mile in advance.

For this reason the best idea is a series of portable, flaming red flares that can be planted by the road or on the shoulder a long distance before other drivers will have to squeeze past your car. Such flares are known as stick flares or fusee flares. You have seen police use them. They are easy to use and astonishingly effective when used properly.

A flame flare looks like this:

It is a long red stick of chemicals tipped with a waterproof paper cover. To light it, grasp the stick in one hand, look for the little cloth tear-tab, then simply rip off the cap. The head of the flare is now exposed; it is a little like the tip of an ordinary kitchen match.

Flare

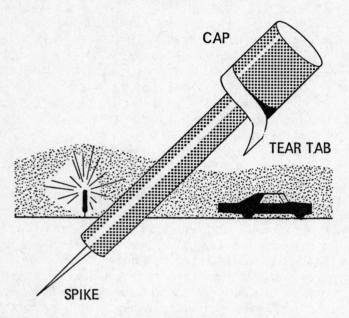

Don't throw the cap away. Save it. This is the striker on which you will light the flare. When the paper cap is torn off, a round, gritty abrasive surface like the side of a matchbox is exposed. Holding the flare away from you, strike this gritty surface briskly against its tip. Be sure to strike away from you and downward, since hot sparks will fly.

Now you can throw the cap away. The flare will light with a brilliant, sputtering red flame and some thin smoke. The smoke is actually extra protection, because for a few moments it shines in the light of the flame and creates a large glowing red cloud. Unfortunately, as flares are made today, this large protective cloud soon dies away; perhaps some day flares will be made that will continue through an emergency to throw off this brilliant warning smoke which can be seen for long distances.

How to "plant" the flares. On any superhighway trip at least three or four flares should be kept within instant reach of the driver, not locked up in the trunk. (Others may be stored there until needed.) Never, however, leave flares in a parked car with playing children.

Take three or four flares under your arm. Ideally you should not hold a flare more than thirty seconds before planting it in the ground. Otherwise hot, molten sparks form and can burn your hands painfully when you do at last hold it upright in order to stick the spiked end in soil. But in a highway emergency it is often wiser to risk the spark burns and carry a lighted flare. Holding the lighted one away from you and slightly below the horizontal, walk quickly back along the road toward approaching traffic. Never wave a flare over your head, because those hot sparks of molten, flaming chemical may fall on your clothing or even on your hair and into your eyes. Try not to let sparks fall on your hand, although, as stated, this sometimes occurs.

However, when hurrying back to flag traffic it is important to wave the flare slowly up and down at arm's length and from waist level downward (to avoid burns). Otherwise, to distant drivers, a flare held in one position appears to be merely the taillight of a moving car. This is especially true after the first protective smoke cloud clears away. In holding any flare even waist high be sure that the wind does not blow sparks horizontally toward your clothing or eyes.

No two emergency situations are ever quite the same. But in general the following is one good procedure for a car stalled on the shoulder very close (within six feet) to the road or with two wheels in the driving lane.

Plant the first flare a short distance behind your car. Lay it flat in the lane if necessary. Some experts prefer to have it about two hundred feet back. Immediately light a second flare and walk it back along the edge of the road toward traffic. Stay on the shoulder. Put this second flare much farther back—perhaps two hundred feet. Now light a third flare and walk it back still farther, preferably at least another two hundred to three hundred feet back. You should now be roughly the length of a city block from your car—or more.

Make special allowance for curves, hillsides, or bridge abutments that may obscure any flares. Try to put flares where they can be seen by all drivers in all lanes! Some police spike flares high up in cracks in fence posts, utility posts, or even trees or roadside embankments. However, the flare farthest back is usually spiked into the soft edge of the road, if it is soft. When spiking a flare into the ground, it is good to wrap the hand in a glove or thick cloth. This protects the hand when sparks are jarred loose by impact.

Flares nearer the car may be spiked into the soft tarry cracks between concrete slabs or simply laid flat on the road near the edge of the lane. Some drivers use small wire flare holders into which flares can be laid without any need for spiking.

If you have brought along a fourth flare, now light it and walk back toward your car, holding it in the hand closest to the traveled lane. If your car is actually blocking one lane, place the flare in mid-lane at least one hundred feet behind your car. It does little good to place a single flare in a lane (as some drivers do) merely ten to twenty feet directly behind a car or truck. This may actually invite drivers to come that far before trying to change lanes. Then in the last-minute confusion several cars may come together violently.

If traffic is light, you may now have fairly good protection. However, if all lanes are running full and traffic is fast, you would be well advised to distribute even more flares—perhaps even farther back than before. But always keep two or three in reserve for further emergency in case police protection fails to arrive before your flares start burning out.

Such an added display of flares should give excellent protection. But never count on this, and never relax your caution. Good as flares are, police have known as many as thirty-five of them to be run down in the wild crush of traffic that moves on some roads at night, especially weekend or holiday nights, when many drivers are rushing home after celebrating.

Don't underestimate the need for several flares. It is not wise to try to rely, as some drivers do, on only one or two flares. Radar tests made by the author, with the New York University Center's Professor W. J. Toth, show that cars on fast super-roads don't slow down materially when only one or two flares are used. They may not even slow down when even half a dozen flares are displayed. But what the flares *do* accomplish is this: When enough flares are lighted in the right place, drivers are alerted to the need for care and they do tend to move out of the blocked lane in time to avoid collision with your car and with each other.

HOW TO CONTROL HEAVY BLEEDING

Medical ideas change. Tourniquets used to be recommended. Then they were found dangerous to use, unless loosened every now and then to restore circulation. Later, as experience with accident victims grew, it was recommended that tourniquets be used only when absolutely necessary and left in place—to be loosened later only in a hospital or by experienced doctors.

Here is the most recent thinking of the Red Cross: Heavy bleeding is controlled by applying direct pressure over the wound with the cleanest material available (sterile gauze is best). Maintain firm pressure until a bandage can be applied. If the bleeding area can be moved without causing additional damage, elevate it. Do not remove the dressing if it becomes saturated; apply more layers of cloth.

In case of an injury when direct pressure and elevation of the injured part fail to control bleeding, press the supplying blood vessel against the underlying bone. This should cause the bleeding to diminish. Meanwhile, direct pressure can be applied. There are only two points on each side of the body where this is of practical use: (1) pressure on the inner half of the arm, midway between elbow and armpit, and (2) pressure applied just below the groin on the front inner half of the thigh.

A tourniquet should be used ONLY for a severe, life-threatening hemorrhage that cannot be controlled by other means.

CHAPTER XXIII

TO SUM IT ALL UP

As STATED IN THE BEGINNING of this book, three main principles must be observed in good driving: (1) It must be considered a quiet art, never a showy skill. (2) You must have a good car. (3) You must know how to deal with emergencies.

To these now may be added several other principles of really expert car-handling:

1. An expert's car moves smoothly and in a perfectly straight line most of the time.

2. Besides giving the usual signals an expert makes his car tell other drivers exactly what its driver plans to do. His car "talks" to other drivers by gradual changes in direction, by the position of its front wheels, by the smoke from its exhaust pipe, by its degree of rocking when brakes are applied, and even by the driver's skillful use of headlights and horn.

3. The expert's car is always surrounded by an ample "space cushion," and its driver is always looking for an "out" in case of emergency.

4. The expert watches the road much farther ahead than ordinary drivers.

5. He also reads the road behind him constantly. He knows nearly as much about what is happening behind him as about what is happening ahead.

6. He adjusts his speed to bad weather and never drives in severe rainstorm or blizzard conditions if he can avoid it.

7. He does not regard the other driver as an idiot or an enemy. He rejects the common notion that most other drivers are stupid or intentionally rude.

8. And he knows that instant danger ahead means instant danger behind and he drives so that he never gets caught in the middle!

THE EXPERT'S SECRETS

THE EXPERT'S SECRETS

HOW TO MAKE YOUR CAR RUN BETTER LONGER

AN EXPERT DRIVER'S CAR is always in top condition. His car's engine lasts longer than most cars' engines. For these reasons, the following recommendations are made. They are expanded from a report that was written by the author for *McCall's* magazine:

Outside my city apartment is a driveway, where I park under a maple tree. The other day my garage man pointed to the roof of my car. It showed traces left by robins that had roosted overhead.

"Droppings," he said, "are your car paint's worst enemy. They can start to eat away a spot in forty-eight hours." He rinsed away the offending stain. "A few more of these will make your new car look old before its time."

From such mechanics, as well as from chemists and engineers, I have learned a half-dozen things you can do to help your car stave off premature old age and eventually bring a greater trade-in allowance.

Drive easily. Today's cars are so lively that it's easy—for men and women alike—to push the gas pedal and roar away in a flash start. We whistle around tight corners and screech to fast stops. Often we are not aware of the strain we cause, because the cars ride so easily; and in the quiet interiors we usually can't hear the tires shrill their warning protests. Too much of this can cut a year or more off your car's life and many dollars off its trade-in value.

Fast starts load an enormous strain on mechanical parts. The stress affects not only your engine but also your transmission, wheels, brakes, and tires. It has been estimated that a single "blast-off" from a traffic light (to beat the driver next to you) costs ten cents in tire wear alone, not to mention the cost in general wear and tear. And a sudden stop, with a short skid-mark attached, costs even more, perhaps even a dollar or two. The skid, like a "blast-off" start, leaves so much melted rubber on the road that you can walk back and feel it.

Sudden turns alone are terribly expensive. For example, some engineers say that using one single expressway cloverleaf turn a day, morning and afternoon, costs a commuting driver the equivalent of a tire a year.

Don't crowd the car ahead. This can be expensive as well as dangerous. The vehicle ahead can pepper your nice, shining car with a steady dulling rain of grit and gravel, thrown back by its wheels. Such debris pits your windshield, nicks the paint above it, and chips paint from the front of your engine hood (where all those bug stains also appear).

Above all, never follow fast sand or gravel trucks or concrete mixers. The falling gravel hits the road, bounces, and shoots at you like bullets. So does gravel flung by truck tires. And I have seen sand, blowing in a stead stream off the top of a fast truck, ruin an expensive windshield in two miles at 50 mph. It etched the glass so badly that the windshield was unsafe for driving.

Be careful where you park. Dents from other people's car doors can make a new car look positively decrepit within a year. No part of your car is safe today from other parkers in those ultranarrow slots marked off on so many streets and lots, where drivers tend to crease your fenders, scratch your sides, and break your taillights.

Your paint job. The tough enamels and lacquers used on cars today are called miracle paints, and for good reason. They are sensationally beautiful. Unlike old paints, which dulled in six months, these will keep their original showroom glitter for several years—but only with your help.

It is imperative to protect your paint not only from bird droppings but also from "fallout," i.e., the clouds of acids, salts, fumes, and smoke that gather over most cities, especially at night when the wind drops. So much fallout can settle on your car's paint that you can *feel* it with your fingertips the next morning. Dew mixes with it to form what chemists call soup, which can damage good paint within a month.

To make your paint last, wax it (or have it waxed) twice a year with good rubbing wax, which resists fallout. Wax it more often if you use easy liquid or spray waves. And even after waxing, rinse fallout from your car on dewy mornings.

To forestall rust, repaint those little nicks as soon as you see them. You can do it yourself. With the tip of a piece of very fine sandpaper, scrape the nick clean, then feather the broken paint edges smooth. Now apply touch-up paint (available from your serviceman or car dealer). It is vital to do this immediately, before any rust can get into the metal.

Keep carpets and mats clean and dry. Rust often spreads underneath them. After driving on salty roads in fall and winter, have someone hose the salt from the paint and chrome. Also have your car hosed *under-*

neath to wash out hidden pockets where wet sand and salt make mud packs. After driving on salt in winter, I always make a special point to do this as soon as I possibly can.

Your engine. Mechanics say that today's engines, if cared for, are good for 100,000 miles without major repairs. Yet some drivers begin to have unnecessary engine trouble in the first or second year, and by the third year a good many engines are ready for overhaul. What often makes the difference is overheating caused by (1) a loose or broken fan belt, which allows your cooling fan to stop turning, (2) broken water hoses, which let the cooling water leak out, or (3) faulty thermostats—the gadgets that are supposed to keep your engine just warm enough. These vital little parts sometimes quit working—and a whole engine can be ruined as a result.

To guard against such automotive migraines, have your serviceman check fan belt, hoses, and thermostat every four months. (Rely on a serviceman you can trust, because a few make a habit of selling unneeded repair parts.)

In case your engine ever does get too hot, learn to watch for the warning signs. If your car has a temperature gauge, glance at it frequently. On some cars a red sentry light is supposed to flash on your dashboard; on others the engine emits a loud buzzing sound. You may smell hot oil, or a passing motorist may point underneath your car because he sees water boiling over. Don't always expect to see steam, which usually shows up only if you happen to stop.

When an engine overheats, a good deal depends on what you do next. Don't make the mistake of trying to keep on driving in order to reach a service station. *Pull safely off the road, stop, and instantly turn off the engine.* Discovered early, an overheated engine may not be badly damaged. But if run even a few moments too long, it can be ruined for good.

THE THREE GREAT SECRETS

Many engines are in trouble at 40,000 miles, some in trouble at 25,000 or occasionally much less. But any good engine should run like a clock for 80,000 or even 100,000 miles.

The reason many drivers don't get this engine life is that they overlook three very simple, but terribly important, protections:

(1) The first secret: the right oil. Oil has always been important, of course, but today the right oil, changed at the right time, almost alone

can decide whether your engine will go 40,000 miles or 100,000 miles without major repairs.

The trick is to use the "MS" (moderate service) oil recommended in your manual—never the low-priced "ML" (light service) oils sometimes sold. These are for lawnmowers, not cars.

Oil will last many thousands of miles, but you may get much better engine service if you change even more often than your manual says, especially if most of your driving is "around town"—i.e., you make many short, stop-and-go trips. These are terribly hard on engines.

And change your oil filter with every other oil change.

On dusty western or southern roads, or in northern states where roads are often heavily over-sanded and over-salted, it does not hurt to change oil every three thousand miles, or even, under extreme conditions, every two thousand.

In western states, after a dust storm drain and replace oil immediately. Don't wait. Don't even go fifty miles.

(2) The second secret: a regular tuneup. Half the cars on the road today are overdue for a tuneup—which means that their owners are heading for repair bills long before those bills should be necessary. It is terribly important to have a tuneup and to clean or change sparkplugs at least once a year.

(3) The third secret: "exercise" your engine. Few drivers realize that engines, like people, need a good brisk physical workout now and then. If you are an around-town driver, your engine quickly loads up with gummy substances and acids, which can actually ruin it.

The best thing you can do for your car, besides keeping good oil in it, is to take it out on a highway once a week for a good "exercise trip" at a speed between 45 and 55 mph. It takes at least a fifteen-mile run for an engine to get good and hot—and heat is exactly what it needs, because heat sweats out those acids and burns out the ruinous deposits.

This is why traveling salesmen often get twice as much mileage from their engines as other drivers do: their long, hot superhighway trips keep their engines burned clean inside. It is a little-known fact that long-trip driving is far easier on engines than slow, around-town use is.

INDEX

INDEX

Accelerator, 26
  and chain collisions, 69
  and G-force, 86
  skidding and, 141, 142
  stuck pedal, 148, 150
Accidents, 151–160
  backing as cause of, 13–14
  blindgating, 41, 42
  dust puff as sign of, 67, 73
  pedestrians and, 18
  signaling at, 60, 152 ff.
  slow drivers and, 96
  speed and, 27, 31
  superhighway, 74, 84
  witnesses, 156–157
  See also Collisions
"Accordion" traffic, 22
Aetna Casualty & Surety Company, viii
Air brakes, 99
Air conditioning, 90, 113
  leak in, 8, 9
  See also Cooling system
Air pressure in tires, 71, 132
Allen, Dr. Merrill L., vii, 48, 49
American Automobile Association, viii, 32
American Trial Lawyers Association, viii
Automatic transmission
  downshift and, 149
  leak in, 7, 8
  and left-foot braking, 23, 91
  and reverse-to-forward lurch, 14
  snow and, 133
  towing and, 156
Axle, leakage from, 9

Backing, 13–14
  and collisions, 69
  in emergencies, 112
  in snow, 129
Backup lights, 112
Baltimore City Police, viii

Bechtold, Grace, viii
Bell System, viii
Bicyclists, 59, 60, 63
Billboards, 86
Bird droppings, 165, 166
Blacktop roads, 111, 117
Blind lanes, 69
Blindgating accidents, 41, 42
Blinkers, 6, 79
  See also Hazard flashers
Blizzards, vi, 128, 161
Blower, 113
Blowouts, 74, 80
Brake lights, 66
  to signal emergency, 58, 69, 73, 84
Brakes
  and automatic transmission, 14, 23, 91
  and control of skidding, 141, 142
  failure of, 23, 148–149, 150
  leak in fluid, 8, 9
  testing, in unfamiliar car, 40
Braking, 22–23
  cadence, 144–145
  and chain collisions, 42, 65–66, 83–84
  for deer, 110
  and G-forces, 86
  in headlight failure, 112
  and "hood-up" emergencies, 4
  left-foot, v, 14, 23, 91–92
  in left turns, 57
  in rain, 117
  seat belt and, 11
  as signal, 73
  "stab-and-steer," 139, 145
  and studded tires, 137
  on superhighway, 75
  at traffic lights, 69
  of unfamiliar cars, 40
Bridges
  icy, 59–60, 74
  shelter under, 124
  on superhighways, 67–68, 74, 76, 84, 86, 87

171